FLOOD WATCH

LANTERN BEACH MYSTERIES, BOOK 2

CHRISTY BARRITT

River Heights

COMPLETE BOOK LIST

Squeaky Clean Mysteries:

While You Were Sweeping, A Riley Thomas Spinoff

The Sierra Files:
#1 Pounced
#2 Hunted
#3 Pranced
#4 Rattled

The Gabby St. Claire Diaries (a Tween Mystery series):
#1 The Curtain Call Caper
#2 The Disappearing Dog Dilemma
#3 The Bungled Bike Burglaries

The Worst Detective Ever
#1 Ready to Fumble
#2 Reign of Error
#3 Safety in Blunders
#4 Join the Flub
#5 Blooper Freak
#6 Flaw Abiding Citizen
#7 Gaffe Out Loud
#8 Joke and Dagger
#9 Wreck the Halls
#10 Glitch and Famous
#11 Not on My Botch

Raven Remington
Relentless

Holly Anna Paladin Mysteries:
#1 Random Acts of Murder
#2 Random Acts of Deceit

Lantern Beach Blackout

   #1 Dark Water

   #2 Safe Harbor

   #3 Ripple Effect

   #4 Rising Tide

Lantern Beach Guardians

   #1 Hide and Seek

   #2 Shock and Awe

   #3 Safe and Sound

Lantern Beach Blackout: The New Recruits

   #1 Rocco

   #2 Axel

   #3 Beckett

   #4 Gabe

Lantern Beach Mayday

   #1 Run Aground

   #2 Dead Reckoning

   #3 Tipping Point

Lantern Beach Blackout: Danger Rising

   #1 Brandon

   #2 Dylan

   #3 Maddox

   #4 Titus

Lantern Beach Christmas

   Silent Night

Crime á la Mode

The Baby Assignment
The Cradle Conspiracy
Trained to Defend
Mountain Survival
Dangerous Mountain Rescue

Nonfiction:

Characters in the Kitchen

Changed: True Stories of Finding God through Christian Music (out of print)

The Novel in Me: The Beginner's Guide to Writing and Publishing a Novel (out of print)

PROLOGUE

CADY MATTHEWS JERKED her eyes open, blanching at the sideways world splayed before her.

Sideways? No, her environment wasn't slanted.

Cady was.

Her face—her entire body, for that matter—pressed with unusual heaviness against a gritty floor. Her pulse pounded dangerously fast, and she was keenly aware of everything going on around her.

Every movement. Every sound. Every pulse of the earth.

Terrifying silence stretched through the chilly air. It was the silence of the unknown. The unseen. The un . . . remembered.

Cady blinked, her eyes and mouth painfully dry.

What was going on? Where was she? Even more, how did she get here?

She scanned the room around her. Wherever she was, the place was dark with only tiny windows atop two walls. The floors were cement and dirty. The walls were a sickly hue of yellow offset by massive water stains.

As Cady glanced out the open door to her left, she realized she was in an office, most likely adjoining an old . . . warehouse? The place appeared to have been abandoned a decade ago based on the grime and odor.

She pushed herself up from her prone position. Her head pounded even harder, the throbs coming with fury.

Something was wrong. Majorly wrong.

The last thing Cady remembered was Raul Sanders pulling up beside her as she walked down the water-logged, dim street after work. He'd ordered her to get into his oversized, blinged-out SUV.

She hadn't wanted to. Hadn't wanted to be anywhere near the leader of DH-7, a notorious gang that instilled fear within people up and down the West Coast. Their reach was rapidly expanding, and with the expansion came trouble. Danger. Death.

But Cady's mission was to bring them down. That was why she'd gone undercover and infiltrated the group. She had hardly slept a wink in the fifty-eight days since the assignment had started. And, as part of her cover, she had to befriend the louse who put money and power above innocent lives. Raul was the most evil man she'd ever met. The world would be safer without him.

Because of the assignment, everything had been stripped away from Cady. Her safe little life was gone. Now each moment felt uncertain. How could she return to normal after this?

She already knew the answer. She couldn't. She'd never be the same when this was over. She only hoped the changes would be worth it.

Cady blinked again, trying to get her thoughts back into focus. Everything blurred around her. Her head felt like gelatin had been stuffed inside, preventing her thoughts from correctly activating.

Raul must have brought her to this place. It was the only thing that made sense. She squinted as she tried to remember.

But she couldn't. Everything was blank—including how much time had passed. That realization caused a shiver to run up her spine and back down again.

Not knowing didn't sit well with her.

One thing she knew for sure: wherever she was, she needed to get out of here.

She braced herself against the floor to push herself up. As she did, she noticed her hands for the first time.

The air drained from her lungs.

Blood. Her hands were covered in blood. Every crevice. The fine lines of her fingerprints. Underneath her nails.

She scrambled to her feet, panic closing in. As she glanced at her shirt, a small cry escaped.

More blood.

Just what had she done?

All Cady knew for certain was that it must be something terrible.

CHAPTER
ONE

TODAY'S GOALS: SELL ICE
CREAM. MIND MY OWN
BUSINESS. STOP DWELLING ON
THE PAST.

CASSIDY LIVINGSTON, known in her previous life as
police detective Cady Matthews, stood on her deck and
stared at the angry gray ocean that surrounded the island
of Lantern Beach, North Carolina. Dark clouds gathered
over the expanse of water in the distance. Meteorologists
had promised a doozy of a storm later today, and if the
horizon was any indicator, they were correct.

Thunderstorms didn't bode well for ice cream sales.
And if Cassidy didn't sell ice cream, she'd be forced to sit
inside her cottage and count the passing minutes until she
could come out of hiding and return home to Seattle. Or
contemplate writing that self-help book. Or look for
another mystery to solve, which might blow her cover.

Those ideas were neither tempting nor wise.

She closed her eyes for a moment as memories
pummeled her. She'd had that dream again last night.
Only it wasn't a dream. It was more memory melded into
a living nightmare.

Every time she remembered the blood on her hands,

she flinched, her muscles tightening so quickly that air rushed from her lungs. The images would never leave her —maybe not until she had answers. Except answers might lead to more nightmares.

If she could only remember . . .

Fear and worry lead only to weakness.

It was one of the quotes from the Day-at-a-Glance inspirational calendar her best friend, Lucy, had given her. Its wisdom was never-ending, and right now it reminded Cassidy that the last thing she needed was to become weak.

Taking another sip of her coffee, she glanced across the street at her neighbor's house, desperate for a distraction from her thoughts. Ty Chambers lived there.

The two of them chatted sometimes, but Cassidy had been making an effort to stay away. Something about the man captured her imagination—and that was the last thing she needed or wanted.

After all, she was dating Ryan Samson, even if she hadn't seen him in more than four weeks. Before that, they'd taken a two-month break while she was undercover with DH-7. Circumstances had caused the divide between them to feel stronger and wider all the time.

But Cassidy had also stayed away because she knew Ty hated liars. When he found out Cassidy wasn't who she'd claimed to be, she wasn't sure if their relationship would survive. Yet she couldn't tell him the truth about who she was or why she was here. She couldn't tell anyone. Only one person knew: Samuel Stephens, the task force head.

With her gaze still angled toward his place, she saw Ty step onto the deck and wave. Cassidy's cheeks heated as she waved back, caught staring. Ty looked like he'd just gotten up, in his white T-shirt and with his messy hair. Of course, his hair was always messy, but that was part of his appeal.

As he leaned against his deck, his muscles flexed. Cassidy's throat clenched when she caught sight of his impressive biceps. She quickly looked away before he caught her staring again.

A few seconds later, her phone buzzed.

It was a text message. From Ty.

> You should secure everything around your house. This storm will bring strong winds.

Well, that was helpful since she hadn't been in Lantern Beach during a storm yet. Her phone buzzed again as Ty continued.

> Tie down the chairs on your deck so they don't fly into your windows.

Cassidy stared at the massive wooden chairs behind her. The last thing she needed was the hassle of her rental being destroyed. She sighed and typed back:

> Do you have any rope I can borrow?

Ty replied right away and told her he'd bring some over in a few minutes.

Perfect. Better yet, Cassidy would meet him. No need making him do all the work. She believed in carrying her weight.

As she rushed down the exterior stairway from her deck, a gust of wind swept over the area, bringing with it a smattering of sand from the massive dunes that separated her place from the beach. It served as an ominous hint of what was to come later when the storm hit full force.

She paused beneath Ty's deck to wait for him. No doubt he'd have to come down here to the little shed under his house to get the rope. As she waited, a chill washed over her. The wind was bringing with it not just sand but also a rush of more temperate air.

All of a sudden, something dripped down on her from above. Was it pouring rain already? She glanced beyond the deck and didn't see any raindrops.

She pulled her shirt to her nose. That smelled like . . . urine?

She looked up, just in time to feel another stream of liquid descend. She gasped and ducked out of the way before it could hit her again.

"Kujo, no!" a deep voice thundered from above her. "Not on the deck, you crazy dog."

Cassidy's mouth opened.

Kujo? You had to be kidding. What kind of dog went to the bathroom on a deck?

Ty pounded down the steps, towing Kujo behind him, and drew to a sudden stop at the bottom. His eyes widened when he saw Cassidy standing there, her hand still on her wet shirt and most likely a look of unconcealed revulsion on her face.

He opened his mouth and then shut it before finally saying, "You didn't . . . Kujo didn't . . .?"

"He just peed on me." Cassidy's stomach churned with disgust.

"I'm so sorry."

Another thought hit her. "Did you know I was down here . . . ?"

He let out a rough, startled chuckle that lasted all of two seconds. "What? No. I would never do that."

Cassidy remembered a few of their past interactions. They'd been heated and unpleasant, to say the least. She thought they'd moved beyond that but . . . "Are you sure?"

"Of course I'm sure. You really think I would let Kujo do that?"

She crossed her arms. "Do you really want me to answer that?"

"For Pete's sake, Cassidy—"

Before he could finish, a car pulled into Ty's driveway, the driver honking incessantly as if announcing himself at a parade. Cassidy and Ty turned toward the vehicle at the same time, their conversation forgotten—at least for now.

"Oh . . . wow." Ty raked a hand through his hair as he stared at the station wagon.

Cassidy froze, temporarily forgetting about the dog pee on her shirt as a man and woman emerged from a modern-day station wagon, excitement oozing from them. They were probably both in their sixties, and their wide smiles made them seem over-the-moon happy.

The woman squealed as she stood at full height, her hands raised in the air and joy written all over her round face. "Tyson Chambers! Aren't you as handsome as ever."

Ty blinked again but took a step closer, the start of a smile forming on his lips. "Mom . . . what a surprise. You're here. From Texas."

As Cassidy's attention fastened on the scene, she stripped off her stained shirt. The blue tank top underneath would be sufficient, and she couldn't stand the thought of sporting urine any longer than necessary. Especially if she was about to meet Ty's parents.

Ty's mom pulled him into a bear hug, squeezing and shaking and letting out sounds someone might use with a baby. Just as she released him, the man—his dad?—took his turn, squeezing Ty so hard that both of their faces turned red.

Ty, who usually seemed so in charge and in control, appeared powerless, as if he was being swept along with the tide.

Cassidy smiled as she watched the scene unfold. It was almost satisfying seeing Ty flustered. The change of pace was nice, especially considering his dog had just peed on her.

Then the man and woman turned toward her with such over-exuberant expressions that Cassidy sucked in a breath and braced herself.

"And you must be his new girlfriend!" Ty's mom let out another squeal and pulled Cassidy into her arms.

Cassidy started to protest, but she couldn't get a word out. The woman's hug smothered Cassidy nearly as much as her rose-scented fragrance.

She glanced over Mrs. Chambers' shoulder in time to see Ty mouth, "I'm so sorry."

Finally, his mom let go. Cassidy was about to explain she wasn't Ty's girlfriend when his dad twirled her around and pulled her into another bear hug.

And here we go again.

"We're so glad to finally meet you," his dad said.

Finally, the surprise hug attack ended, and Cassidy gulped in a deep breath before launching into an explana-

tion about who she was. She had to set the record straight.
Pronto.

"It's nice to meet you, but I'm actually—"

Before she could finish, Ty's arm went around her waist,
and he pulled her close—intimately close. "This is Cassidy."

What was he doing? What in the world was going on
here? Mr. I-Hate-Liars was lying? Right?

Her gut twisted at the conundrum.

"It's so wonderful to meet you!" His mom's face absolutely glowed as her gaze bounced back and forth between
the two of them. "You can call me Del, and this is Frank."

Del had a round face and dark brown hair cut to her
chin. She was about forty pounds overweight, but the
main thing Cassidy noticed was her bright smile.

Frank had a broad build with the start of a paunch in
his midsection. He hardly had any hair, and what he did
have—mostly around the sides—was shaved short. He
had Ty's warm eyes and angular features.

As they bent to greet Kujo, Ty leaned close—close
enough that his breath tickled Cassidy's ear. Close enough
that his parents couldn't see his lips move. "You owe me
one, remember?"

Cassidy did owe him. She'd also begged him to play
along with her a few weeks ago when she needed a cover
because someone from her past had arrived in town.

But . . . But that had been different. Right? Yet—

She released her breath—and tried to release her stub-
born conviction.

This was going to be painful, but Cassidy would
swallow her pride. Ty had done it for her. But he better
have a good explanation.

"It's so nice to meet you," she finally said.

"What brings you out this way?" Ty asked, his arm still draped around Cassidy's waist. "It's quite the surprise."

His mom clapped. "That's just what we wanted—to surprise you."

"Well, it worked."

"We missed you, and, since it's summer, we decided to pack up and come visit for a week," his dad said.

Ty tensed beside her. "A week? Wow."

"Your father is retired now. We have all the time in the world to do whatever we want. Like come see you whenever we want!"

This was getting more entertaining by the minute.

"Let me help you bring your luggage upstairs," Ty said. "You must be tired."

"We are," Del said. "We haven't pulled an all-nighter in quite a while."

"You drove all night?" Ty released his arm from around Cassidy and walked toward the station wagon.

For some strange reason, Cassidy missed his touch. Missed the weight of his arm against her back. Missed the warmth coming from his body.

Which was stupid.

Cassidy helped Ty carry some suitcases upstairs. She'd hoped for a minute alone with him, but his parents had followed. As they trotted back downstairs to retrieve more bags—this time, groceries they'd brought with them—another car pulled up.

It was a circus around here.

To her surprise, Skye rushed out from the driver's seat, tears flowing from her eyes. Her lithe body bent with distress as the wind swept her long dark hair into her face, making it collide with her wet cheeks.

Cassidy's heart thumped into her throat. Something was seriously wrong.

"Ty, I need your help." Skye flipped her hair from her face, revealing eyes full of agony and worry.

"What's going on?" Ty stepped closer, his shoulder muscles visibly tightening.

"I was arguing with a man, and now he's disappeared, and the police think foul play may be involved." She stopped long enough to suck in a deep breath of air. "And they think I might somehow be a part of it. Please, help!"

CHAPTER
TWO

CASSIDY'S PULSE throbbed as she waited to hear more. It took every ounce of her self-control not to snap into cop mode. Instead, she tried to appear laid-back and easygoing, just like her ice cream-selling persona required.

Ty squeezed Skye's arm and lowered his voice. "Start from the beginning. What happened?"

Skye pinched the skin between her eyes and lowered her head—classic signs of distress. The gypsy-spirited beach lover never seemed stressed, so something must be seriously wrong.

"I've been arguing with that new produce stand owner in town," Skye started. "He set up right across the street from me, and he's stealing my business."

Cassidy had noticed the new guy while she was on her ice cream route and had thought it was dirty to set up so close to Skye's van stand, as she called it. Her friend had crafted her storefront out of an old hippie van and added a pergola.

"I mean, I know they say competition is good for business, but not on an island this size." Skye's voice sounded thin and cracked with every other word. "We had some pretty heated discussions."

Cassidy waited, anxious to hear where this was going.

"Anyway, he sent a spy over to check out my inventory, and then he priced everything at least twenty-five cents lower," Skye said. "Bower Wilson told me about it. He overheard them while he was fishing down at the inlet. Anyway, I went to his house to confront Buddy Macklemore—that's the name of the owner. When I got to his place, I knocked, and the door opened. There was blood inside. The police just happened to show up while I was standing there, and they assumed I had something to do with it."

Ty squinted. "Was there a body?"

Skye swung her head back and forth. "No, there wasn't. But something . . . something . . . violent happened there. I just know it." A sob escaped her.

"It doesn't sound like the police have enough to hold you," Cassidy said, quickly reminding herself to act like a novice. "I mean, from what I understand about police investigations, which is hardly anything, obviously."

"They don't. Not yet. But they're searching for Buddy and advised me not to leave town." Another sob escaped from Skye. "What am I going to do?"

Cassidy and Ty exchanged a glance.

"We'll help you get through this." Ty wrapped an arm around Skye's shoulders. "Let's not assume the worst. It's like Cassidy said—it doesn't sound like there's enough to hold you."

She sniffled. "I just have a bad feeling about this."

"What do you need us to do?" Ty asked.

Skye shook her head. "I don't know. I'm afraid Chief Bozo is going to arrest me. Even I think I look guilty."

His name was really Chief Bozeman, but a lot of people called him Chief Bozoman or Chief Bozo behind his back. He'd rightfully earned the nickname and reputation on pure incompetence.

"Again, until they find a body, you should be okay," Cassidy said. "I mean, I think. Sue Grafton says that's the way it works."

She inwardly cringed. She so much wanted to lend her expertise, but she couldn't give people a clue about her prior life. It was too dangerous, too risky, and entirely frustrating.

"She's right," Ty said. "I don't think they can charge you with anything right now."

"Maybe Mac has some information he would share," Cassidy said.

Mac Macarthur was the former police chief here in town, and he'd become both a friend and an entertaining commentator on life in Lantern Beach. He and Cassidy often chatted over lunch at the Crazy Chefette.

"That's a great idea," Ty said.

"I can go talk to him." Cassidy was anxious to get away from whatever madness had ensued upon Ty's life. On the other hand, she really wanted to talk to Ty and discover what this story was. Later.

"I'll go with you." Ty nodded, as if the decision had been made.

"But your family . . ." Cassidy said, remembering Del and Frank upstairs.

"They're exhausted from their all-night drive and want

to get some rest. I'll talk to them to confirm, but they should be okay."

"What about me?" Skye looked back and forth from Ty to Cassidy.

"The best thing you can do is lie low," Ty said. "Stay far away from whatever's happening."

She squeezed her eyes shut. "I can't even work today. There's a storm coming in."

Cassidy knew the feeling. She couldn't either. It was a good thing her one and only employee—Skye's niece Serena—was up in Michigan to be a bridesmaid in a wedding. At least she wouldn't feel guilty about not having any money to pay her part-time employee.

"Why don't you stay at my place?" Cassidy said. "No one will find you there, so it will give you the chance to collect your thoughts."

Why had Cassidy offered that? Having someone in her cottage was a terrible idea. What if Skye got nosy and found her hidden stash of guns?

No, Cassidy had been careful. There was no other evidence of her past life at the cottage.

Skye's eyes lit. "Could I? That would be great."

"Will you be okay by yourself?" Ty asked.

"I'll call Lisa and see if she can leave the restaurant for a while. If she can't, I'll call Austin. Certainly, someone's available."

"They'll make the time for you, Skye." Ty nodded toward the stairs. "Let me go talk to my folks. I'll be right back."

As soon as Ty stepped away, Cassidy turned to Skye, grateful for a moment alone with her. Ty was far too observant, too smart. She couldn't let the man figure out her secrets, and she always felt like he was on the verge of doing just that.

"Tell me more about this guy whose house you went to —starting with where he was staying and how you knew his location," Cassidy said.

Skye sucked in a shaky breath and turned away from another smattering of wind-driven sand. "His name is Buddy Macklemore. He's from New York. He was staying on Sea Oat Drive in one of those big houses on the ocean."

"Two questions. First, how did you know where he's staying?"

Skye's cheeks turned red. "I followed him one day. But it's not like it sounds. I just wanted to know where he was in case I ever needed to talk to him."

Not like it sounds? Cassidy hoped that was true because it sounded like Skye had it out for him. Cassidy didn't say that aloud, though.

"Second question: how can he afford to stay in a house like that?" According to Skye, she barely made enough money selling produce to stay in her 1970s RV at the local campground. A large house like that didn't fit with the facts.

"I have no idea. Certainly, his fruit and vegetable stand wasn't *that* profitable. However, he had all the bells and whistles at his place. That nice sign and the custom building. It just didn't add up to me. I mean, if you already have money, why start a business like this here in town?"

"That's a great question." A produce stand on an island with seasonal tourism wasn't a recipe for success and sudden wealth.

"From what I can tell, he didn't have any family. At least they weren't here with him. He was one of those boisterous guys, the kind who are great salesmen. The locals would still buy from me—I had their loyalty. But the vacationers? Of course, they're going to gravitate toward a place that looks more together than my hippie van."

As if to state her agreement, Elsa—the ice cream truck —began playing "Apples and Bananas."

Cassidy sighed. That truck seemed to have a mind of her own—and it was always at the worst possible time.

————

Ten minutes later, Ty and Cassidy left. Ty had quickly secured the items on her deck before they departed, insisting she would regret it later if they didn't.

They bounced down the road in his truck. Ty had finally gotten his own vehicle back, and it was a beauty—a 1958 Chevy 3100 with a V-8 engine. He'd kept the original teal color and chrome accessories. Cassidy had fallen in love at first sight—with the truck, not with Ty.

As she gazed out the window at the gray skies around them, Cassidy desperately wanted to ask why Ty had lied to his parents. He must have a good reason. But those questions would have to wait. They had more pressing concerns right now.

Important things come first. More wisdom left behind by Lucy.

"Skye seems pretty shaken," Cassidy started.

"I can't blame her. It's not every day people see stuff like that. I know I'll never forget the things I saw while deployed."

He didn't talk about his time as a Navy SEAL very often, but Cassidy was curious about his time overseas.

Something life-changing—maybe many things—had happened, but she had no idea what.

"There are some things you see that become a part of you."

Ty stole a glance at her. "You sound like you speak from experience."

She shrugged, realizing she was treading in dangerous waters. "You can say that."

"Does it go back to that incident with flakka?"

Cassidy had told Ty she'd been abducted by DH-7, injected with the drug, and that she'd awakened with a lightning tattoo—DH-7's trademark. The story had strains of truth to it, so Cassidy had gone with it.

She nodded, not faking the heaviness that washed over her. "Yeah, unfortunately."

Her words were true. She'd been a detective for five years, but those two months undercover superseded all her other experiences. It was a darkness in her life that she feared would never fade.

She thought she'd feel satisfaction in her role at breaking the gang apart. Instead, she only felt emptier at the scope of evil she'd seen. Evil she didn't know was possible.

And that bothered her.

Ty pulled to a stop in front of Mac's house. It was just down the street. Of course, on an island this size, everything was just down the street.

Unless you wanted to leave the island.

There were no bridges to the mainland—only ferries, and you needed an abundance of patience when following their pre-set schedule. It was part of the reason Cassidy had come here. It was secluded—and safe.

Well, mostly safe. Supposedly.

Just as they stepped out of Ty's truck, a loud boom sounded nearby. They glanced at each other.

"That didn't sound good," Ty said, concern etched on his features.

They both darted into his backyard to find Mac leaning over something that looked like a . . . bomb.

CHAPTER
THREE

CASSIDY'S HEART raced as she stopped in her tracks, unwilling to move any closer. "Mac, maybe you shouldn't do that . . ."

He glanced up and smiled, his friendly face glowing. "Cassidy! Great to see you here. You too, Ty."

He continued to fiddle with some wires, a floppy olive-colored hat covering his fair skin and white hair.

"Mac, what are you doing?" Tension still stained Ty's voice as he stared at the scene in front of him.

He waved his hand in the air. "I'm just practicing defusing a bomb. Gotta keep my skills up-to-date."

That was Mac for you. Cassidy had seen him rappelling down the side of his house already. But a bomb?

"Is that a good idea?" Cassidy wondered how she could step in and defuse this situation—and maybe the bomb as well.

"Well, it's not a real bomb. Of course."

Ty shifted. "What was that boom we heard?"

"Sound effect." A smile tugged at Mac's lips as he glanced up. "They help keep me on my toes. I put the effects on a timer, but I never look at the countdown. So it goes off, and the sound surprises even me."

Brilliant on his part. Scary for anyone who didn't know what was going on.

Mac stood and brushed the sand from his knees. "I suppose you're not here to talk about this."

Cassidy shook her head, remembering the reason they'd come. Skye's tear-stained face flashed through her mind. "We need your help."

His eyes brightened. "I always like to help. What's going on?"

He abandoned his bomb and stepped toward them, slipping into the shade and out of the sun, which volleyed in and out of the clouds as the storm continued to whisk closer.

"Someone is missing," Ty said. "There's blood all over his rental house, and our friend is apparently a suspect."

"Not sure what I can do. Sorry for your friend, though. Why does Bozoman suspect your friend?"

"She was at the house when the police arrived," Cassidy said. "They'd been arguing, so they think she has motive."

"I can understand that. Who tipped the police off? Why'd they go to the house?"

"Those are great questions," Cassidy said. "We don't know. Nor do we know how to find out."

"Come inside." He motioned for them to follow. "Let's listen to the scanner."

"But this would have happened more than an hour ago," Cassidy said, not sure his plan would work.

"I record stuff."

Cassidy was impressed. She wasn't aware that people could do that. Nor that people would want to, but if it worked to their advantage . . .

They followed him inside his place. It was a simple little cottage, complete with police memorabilia from his time as chief. Pictures of Mac with famous celebrities who'd come into town adorned the walls, along with some hunting rifles and stuffed fish and deer heads.

All in all, the entire place screamed Mac.

Cassidy wondered for a minute if he'd ever been married or if he'd always been a bachelor. She'd have to find those things out later—if Mac was willing to share. There was still so much she didn't know about him.

He sat down at a thick desk pushed against the living room wall and pulled out some kind of rectangular box the size of a TV remote control. He played with a few buttons and then hit Play.

Ty and Cassidy stood behind him, waiting anxiously to hear what he found. Sure enough, an hour-and-a-half ago a call went out.

"We've got a 10-62 on a house on Sea Oats," the dispatcher said. "It's at 202384."

Chief Bozeman's voice came on the line. "Any more details?"

"A neighbor reported a break-in that's in progress."

"Details on this neighbor?"

"He was anonymous and didn't wish to leave his name. Didn't want to start trouble, he said."

"I'm on my way."

Mac hit stop and then twirled in his office chair to face them. "I guess that wasn't much help."

"Are anonymous tips typical for things like this?" Ty asked.

Mac shrugged. "Fairly. People don't want to be seen as a snitch, especially if they're uncertain about the outcome."

"It seems like it would be unusual for someone to call the police on Skye, though," Cassidy said, her mind whirling. "I mean, she said the front door was unlocked so she stepped inside. The average Joe passing by wouldn't think she was breaking in. Most people around here are vacationers, after all, so it's not like they would recognize that she didn't live there."

"Maybe you should double-check with your friend and see if her story matches up." Mac shrugged, but his eyes made it obvious he thought there was more to the story.

"It's not a bad idea," Ty said. "Skye was awfully frantic when she talked to us. Maybe she left a detail out."

"It wouldn't hurt to question some of the neighbors also and ask if they saw anything," Cassidy said. "I mean, that makes sense to me."

"Let me guess." Ty grinned. "Sue Grafton?"

"Of course," Cassidy responded lightly. She needed to read more of Kinsey Millhone and the Alphabet series, just in case anyone ever tried to discuss plot points with her. She couldn't let a mystery novel series—one she claimed to have read but hadn't—blow her cover.

"I'm telling you." Mac clamped his hand on Cassidy's shoulder. "This girl has the chops to be a top-notch investigator. The way she solved that last murder here on the island . . . it was one for the books. Very Perry Mason-like."

"I don't know what you're talking about. It was all

Chief Bozeman. I just had to pry the answers out of him."
In reality, Cassidy had utilized every ounce of her acting
skills to pull it off without drawing attention to herself.

Mac grunted, and Cassidy could tell he didn't believe
her.

"I can say this," he continued. "I know the guy who
owns the house at 202384 Sea Oats. As soon as the scene is
cleared, how about we all go take a look?"

Excitement surged through Cassidy, but she tried to
tamp it down. "I've never seen a crime scene before. But as
long as I'm with y'all, I think I'll be okay."

She threw the "y'all" in because she was supposed to
be from Texas. An old classmate who'd moved from Texas
to Seattle had always talked like that, so she used it every
once in a while to hopefully solidify her cover.

"That sounds great," Ty said. "Call us. I know Skye is
freaked out, so anything we can do to put her at ease
would be appreciated."

———

Once Cassidy and Ty were back in his truck, they made no
effort to leave. Instead they sat there, each processing their
own thoughts.

"I guess there's nothing else we can do at this point,"
Ty said. "Questioning the neighbors while the police are
most likely processing the scene seems like a bad idea."

"I agree. If we do that, we should wait until later so we
don't raise suspicions. I guess we should go check on Skye
in the meantime."

"Sounds like a plan." He cranked his engine.

Cassidy knew this was her chance to ask Ty the other

questions that had been pressing on her. He wasn't getting out of this that easily.

She crossed her arms. "You ready to tell me why I'm your girlfriend?"

As he sighed, a pallor came over him and he put the truck back into Park. He rolled his window down to let some of the frisky breeze from the approaching storm cool them.

"I'm sorry about that," he started, rubbing his neck. "I shouldn't have placed you in that position. I panicked."

"I didn't think you ever panicked." Navy SEALs didn't panic, did they?

He shrugged and stared out the window, all of his features tight with stress. "I suppose I do when it comes to the people I love."

"Would you mind starting at the beginning? Because I don't know what pretending to be your girlfriend has to do with the people you love."

He ran a hand over his face and turned toward her. His brown eyes pleaded with her to understand. But she saw another emotion there too. Grief.

"My mom has battled cancer for the past ten years," he started. "Ovarian. She was in recovery and then it came back, and now she's in recovery again. In the middle of that, I was stationed in the Middle East, which is very stressful for any parent to have a child over there. And, as if that wasn't enough, my younger brother got caught up with the wrong crowd. Started doing drugs and pretty much shut us out of his life."

Against her better instincts, Cassidy reached over and squeezed his arm. His story was surprising . . . and gut-wrenching. "I'm so sorry, Ty."

"Yeah, it's been a tough several years for my family. And my mom . . . well, she can't seem to catch a break."

"And this is where your 'girlfriend' comes in?" Cassidy kept her voice soft, realizing how much pain this conversation must be churning up.

"My mom likes to worry about me—like any good mother, I guess. When she called me a few months ago, I told her I'd met a girl."

"But you hadn't?"

Ty shook his head. "No, I did meet someone—her name was Sarah—and I went on a few dates with her. But she was only here on vacation and left at the end of her two weeks. It was fun, but we both knew it was nothing more. We didn't have a strong enough connection to keep it going long-distance."

His words caused an unidentifiable emotion to rise in Cassidy. Satisfaction? Jealousy? Curiosity? She wasn't sure.

"Anyway, when I told my mom I'd finally gone on a date again, she was so happy. I mean, over the moon. She thinks everyone should be happily married like she and my father are. I know this might sound strange, but it made me feel like I was doing something positive for her. It's crazy, but I thought maybe she could finally relax and enjoy herself if she wasn't worrying about me."

"I suppose I can see that." It seemed like the whole charade had started as a considerate gesture. But how had that gesture turned so wrong?

"I realize there's such a thing as a lie of omission, and I hate lies. I really hate them."

"I remember that." How could she forget? Cassidy was living one herself.

"But I didn't bother to correct her. I figured I'd tell her eventually. But when she got out of the car today . . . she looked so happy. We know the chances of this cancer coming back are likely, Cassidy. I just wanted to allow her some joy in the moment. I never should have pulled you into it."

Her mind raced. She wasn't Cady Matthews here. She was Cassidy Livingston. And with her new identity, she needed to be all in. She wouldn't do anything to compromise her standards, but she could . . .

"How about this? For the week they're here, you and I are dating," Cassidy said.

Ty's voice rose in pitch as he turned to her. "Really?"

"Really. Then you won't be lying, and your mom can enjoy herself."

"You would do that for me?" His eyebrows jammed together in doubt.

"It's kind of sweet that you're looking out for your mom like that." They said how a man treated his mom was the way he'd treat his wife one day. That meant Ty would bend over backward to make some woman happy. Someone was going to be a very lucky lady.

"Thank you, Cassidy. That . . . that means a lot to me. More than you know."

She shrugged like it wasn't a big deal. What was one more story in her already long list of hidden truths? "I mean, as long as when this is done we can go back to not liking each other."

He grinned. "Absolutely."

She wagged a finger at him. "And no funny business."

"I wouldn't dream of it. Besides, I like brunettes. Quiet ones. With short hair."

Why did that both disappoint and delight Cassidy? Disappoint because she was a blonde and delight because she was really a brunette? It didn't matter because there wasn't anything between them, and there never would be.

"Now, let's get back to Skye." Cassidy patted his cheek. ". . . sweetheart."

CHAPTER
FOUR

TY KEPT REPLAYING Cassidy's surprise offer.

In his gut, he didn't feel good about deceiving his mom. He knew better than to lie. But seeing his mom smile again was worth it. And, it was like Cassidy said, they were dating now. Even if it was as a ruse.

He wrestled with the thoughts as he pulled up to Cassidy's house. He'd have to have a long talk with God about this later. And he'd have to have a long talk with himself, as well, because something about the idea of dating Cassidy brought him more delight than necessary.

Women were just trouble, and he'd be wise to remember that. He'd already had his heart broken once—by his ex-fiancée—and he planned to stay single for a long, long time as a result. That would not make his mom feel any better, however.

With Cassidy by his side, they climbed the steps to her place and saw Austin, Lisa, and Skye were all there, sitting in a circle in the living room area. Skye's face was still red and puffy, and everyone else seemed somber as well.

Skye's face perked when they walked in, and she jumped to her feet. "Well?"

"Whoever reported you was anonymous." Ty paused just inside the door. "But Chief Mac knows the owner of the house. As soon as the police release the crime scene, he's going to let us go in."

"How will that help?" Skye wrung her hands together, appearing on the verge of collapse.

"We may find something that will indicate what happened," Ty said, finding a strange strength in having Cassidy beside him. "If Buddy is . . . dead . . . maybe we'll find something to indicate why someone would kill him."

Skye sank back on the couch, and Austin slid an arm around her shoulders. "Like what? And wouldn't the police have found something there?"

"It's hard to say," Ty told her. "They could have missed something. Maybe letters or photos."

Ty's stomach clenched as Skye's face turned even paler. There was something she wasn't telling them.

"What is it?" Ty prodded.

She buried her face in her hands. "I wrote him some letters. Nasty letters."

Cassidy exchanged a look with Ty before asking, "What did these letters say?"

"That I hoped he died." Skye released a half moan, half cry.

Ty's stomach clenched tighter. "That's not good."

"I know! We even talked about keeping our anger in check at Bible study last week. I don't know what got into me. I was just so mad. I haven't been this angry in a long time. I mean, I've really been working on controlling my temper, but the passionate side of me overpowered the temperate side and . . ."

Cassidy knelt in front of Skye and kept her voice low. "Did you do anything to indicate you broke in, Skye? Were there any reasons someone would call the police? You said earlier you knocked and the door opened, that it wasn't latched."

Skye's face slipped to an even paler shade of white. "Well, I may have pounded on his door and shouted for him to come outside."

"What was so urgent that you needed to confront him right then and there?" Ty left his post by the door and moved toward the couch, closer to Skye and Cassidy.

"I found out about that spy he'd sent over to my stand. I wanted to tell him what I thought about his dirty tactics."

Ty glanced around the room, desperately wishing he could help his friend. Chief Bozeman probably wouldn't do Skye any favors. The man was a bumbling idiot most of the time.

He hadn't wanted to believe that, but the facts had stacked up and proven it over and over again.

"Has anyone else had any encounters with this man?" Ty asked, feeling like he was at one of his strategic planning meetings he had as a SEAL before any big mission.

The rest of the gang shook their heads.

"How about a picture?" Ty said. "I need to know what Buddy Macklemore looks like. Especially if he's still alive."

Cassidy hurried over to the desktop computer set up in the corner. She typed in a few things and then leaned back so everyone could see the screen. "Here he is."

Buddy's picture stared back at him. The man was probably in his late forties. He had a prominent double chin, ginger hair, and dancing green eyes. He appeared to carry thirty extra pounds but, based on the grin on his face, that didn't bother him.

"Anything else about him online?" Ty asked, stepping closer to Cassidy.

"It says here on his social media page that he's from Buffalo, New York. He owned his own business up there." Cassidy squinted at the screen. "It looks like an electronics business, but I can't be sure. I don't see any mention of a spouse or children, but he does look like an all-around social guy. He has a lot of pictures of himself with a lot of different people—at restaurants, parties, ball games, etc."

"Any connections between him and this area?" Ty moved a stack of Sue Grafton novels from the heavy end table and leaned against it. "That's what I'm curious about. Why did he choose Lantern Beach of all places to come set up shop?"

Cassidy typed a few more things in, her slender fingers flying over the keyboard. "No, I don't see anything. He hasn't even mentioned his new fruit stand. Wait." She paused. "Wait, this is weird."

"What is it?" Ty leaned closer.

"He actually has two pages on Facebook," Cassidy said. "One is under Buddy Macklemore, but the other is under Big Buds. He was tagged twice in one of these pictures. That's the only way I know. When I go to this other site, he mentions the produce stand and coming to Lantern Beach. He calls the island Paradise and says he's living the life finally."

"It's not entirely unusual for people to give up everything and come here," Lisa said. "That's what I did."

She'd given up her career as a scientist to become a chef specializing in weird food combinations.

"But you'd been here before," Ty said. "You vacationed here as a child."

"It's true, but it's still not unusual." Lisa shrugged. "Everyone fantasizes about island life."

"We need to find out who else Buddy knew around here and see if they can tell us why exactly he came to Lantern Beach," Ty said. "If there is a good reason. Everyone, keep your eyes and ears open around town. We all know how people talk."

Before he could say anything more, his phone buzzed. It was his mom, and she wanted to take him and Cassidy to lunch.

Ty was jumping from one problem to another. Except this second problem he'd created himself.

Cassidy had been in the car with Del Chambers for only five minutes, and she was already fascinated by the woman.

Whereas Ty was reserved and purposeful, Del . . . she laughed easily. Boisterously. And she seemed so happy, just like Ty had said.

Did that mean she wasn't always like this? Had cancer and the estrangement of her son stripped her of joy for a season?

Ty sat beside Cassidy in the backseat of the station wagon, his arm draped across the back of the seat. Cassidy knew he still wasn't comfortable with the deception, and she had to admire that about him. Some people lied without a second thought, which made them the scariest kind of liars. At least Ty felt bad about it.

Del talked about how beautiful the area was and about how much she'd enjoyed the drive here and how many memories the cottage brought back to her. From what Cassidy gathered, the house had once belonged to Del's father, and she'd spent many summers here while growing up.

Cassidy enjoyed the opportunity to listen, especially since she was having trouble gravitating her thoughts away from Skye and the situation with Buddy.

Finally, they pulled up to a small restaurant called The Docks, located on the water right off a little boardwalk area in town. Even though the weather might turn bad at any minute, Ty's parents insisted on eating outside, and they got a table on the patio overlooking the water.

The whole area downtown was quaint and lovely. Beside the ocean was a wooden boardwalk with benches, swings, and little shower and rinsing areas. The first line of shops and restaurants stretched parallel to that board-walk, followed by another sidewalk and then another row of restaurants and shops. A few little amusement-type rides like a miniature Ferris wheel and a carousel were a little farther down, and in the far distance an abandoned lighthouse stood guard over all of it.

The scent of approaching rain mixed with the salty smell of the ocean, as well as the spicy Old Bay seasoning from the steamed shrimp dish being devoured at a nearby table. There wasn't a more perfect scent combination. Not to Cassidy. Not at this moment, at least.

In her month of living in Lantern Beach, Cassidy hadn't eaten here yet, but she'd heard good things about the place. Carter Denver, the town's local singer/song-writer, played "Somewhere Over the Rainbow" in the background, his earthy voice setting the tone for the meal. Every time Carter showed up, he seemed to set the perfect soundtrack for Cassidy's day.

It was one more thing to love about this town.

After they'd ordered, Del turned to Cassidy, her eyes sparkling with curiosity. "So, tell me how the two of you met. I can't wait to hear this story."

Cassidy and Ty exchanged a look. This was going to be interesting.

Cassidy decided to let Ty take the lead. It was the least she could do since Ty had gotten them into this mess.

He took a long sip of his water before clearing his throat. "It's actually kind of funny. I was driving Ralph's old truck. I thought Cassidy was letting me into traffic, but she wasn't. We both stopped at a grocery store, and she gave me a verbal lashing for cutting her off."

Del's wide-eyed gaze turned to her as she waited to hear Cassidy's side.

Cassidy nodded. Ty had gone with the truth—that was exactly the way they'd met. Hearing it out loud made her feel a touch unbalanced, though. Cassidy usually tried to take care with her words, but that day she'd been stressed and sleep-deprived after driving more than fifty hours from Seattle.

"I saw the stickers on the back of the truck and jumped to some incorrect conclusions," Cassidy admitted.

She held her breath, waiting to see if Del would release any mama bear fury. "Well, I would too. Those stickers on the back of Ralph's truck are disgraceful. Every time I see him, I tell him so. I'm surprised Ty was even driving it."

"I was helping him fix it, so we traded vehicles for a couple weeks," Ty said.

"I don't blame Cassidy one bit," Frank said. "I'd say she was using good judgment. Besides, I like a woman who speaks her mind."

Cassidy offered a soft smile. At least there was that.

"Then it turned out we're neighbors," Cassidy continued, sharing a smile with Ty.

"And I quickly learned to never sneak up on her," Ty added. "I accidentally did that once, and she flipped me over her shoulder."

Cassidy shrugged. "What can I say? Those self-defense classes paid off."

Del laughed. "Oh, you two. I can just see you're perfect for each other. I've always said Ty needs someone who isn't afraid to stand up to him."

"You make me sound scary, Mom."

"Oh, not scary. Intimidating. I mean, you're a former Navy SEAL. Even your size could be considered imposing. Plus you're so handsome." She squeezed his cheek.

"Mom . . ." Ty's cheeks turned red.

It was adorable.

Cassidy held back a smile, not letting it go unnoticed that Ty turned the conversation to fishing.

As she sat back and listened, she realized they did sound like a couple. It was . . . strangely normal and spotlighted an emptiness she hadn't realized was there.

Their food was delivered, pulling Cassidy from her thoughts. She had gotten grilled tuna with a side salad, while Ty and his family had ordered crab-cake sandwiches and fries.

As she ate, her gaze wandered to the crowds on the

sidewalks just beyond the fenced-off outdoor dining area. Mostly families, with groups of college friends and senior adults mixed in there.

Her eyes narrowed when she saw a familiar face in the distance. A semi-familiar face, at least. She'd caught a glance for only a second before the man darted into a gift shop.

Was that . . . ?

The man had looked like Buddy. Same ginger hair. Same basic build. Same ruddy skin.

Cassidy stood and wiped her mouth. "Would you excuse me a minute? I need to run to the restroom."

She couldn't sit here and do nothing. Not when she might have just spotted her best lead.

CHAPTER
FIVE

CASSIDY CONTROLLED HER PACE, trying not to tip anyone off as she hurried from the area. She bypassed the bathroom, though, and headed out the front door instead. With one last glance behind her—to make sure Ty hadn't spotted her—she hurried across the sidewalk.

She had to see if she was correct.

She wound her way through the crowds, slipped into the gift shop, and paused.

The store was packed with wall-to-wall merchandise and shoppers who'd forgone the beach for indoor activities.

She started to weave her way down the aisles when someone stepped out in front of her. A teenager wearing a navy blue "Happy Beach" vest and a braces-laden, sales-man-worthy smile.

"Can I help you?"

Cassidy offered a fleeting smile and peered behind him, hoping he'd get the hint. "No, I'm just looking."

She tried to skirt around him, but he pushed his way in

front of her again. "Are you sure? I can point you to some great souvenirs. Like this beauty—buy two and get one half off."

He held up a yellow foam can cooler with Lantern Beach printed on it.

Irritation burned in Cassidy, and she craned her neck, desperate not to lose the man. "I'll find you if I need help. Thank you."

She started forward again when the boy weaseled his way in front of her and blocked her path yet again.

This time, she didn't stop to continue the conversation. She pushed past him, determined not to let this guy get away.

She rushed past the T-shirts and the beach towels and the keychains and every other souvenir imaginable. They were all plastered with Lantern Beach, even though every other gift shop up and down the East Coast had the same items, only with their distinct destination on them. Myrtle Beach. Ocean City. Hilton Head.

Cassidy didn't see the man.

Where could he have gone?

She pushed forward until she reached the back of the store. When she got there, her stomach dropped.

This wasn't the back of the store. The place had two entrances.

The man must have gone out the back.

Cassidy let out a sigh as she realized the Buddy looka-like had probably gotten away. So much for that lead.

———

Cassidy checked the sidewalk outside the other entrance, just in case. But she already knew the man was long gone, and it was all that Happy Beach employee's fault.

Before she returned to the restaurant, she paused a moment and sucked in a deep breath. She had to compose herself.

Why did she feel so strongly about helping Skye? In her gut, Cassidy knew it was about more than finding justice—though that was a huge reason and an attribute woven deep into the fibers of her being.

Cassidy knew what it felt like to unwittingly find yourself in the middle of a possible crime.

Her mind flashed back to that day she'd woken up in a dirty warehouse with blood on her hands. The moment still haunted her every day. Every night.

Maybe her soul wouldn't be at peace until she had some answers.

But it was hard to get answers about her own nightmare when she was on the other side of the country.

So much had changed since that assignment with DH-7. If Cassidy could go back, sometimes she thought she would refuse to take it. That she should have continued on with her safe, normal life, where her biggest worry was her family's displeasure with her career choice.

But then Raul would still be alive. DH-7 would be growing stronger. The gang would still be hurting people and distributing a deadly version of the psychotic-episode-inducing drug flakka. She hadn't stopped the gang, but she'd slowed them down. It was something.

When the case went to trial, she hoped to further fracture the deadly gang's infrastructure. They were a growing menace, and the world would be better off without them.

And sometimes, sacrificing yourself for the greater good was the only choice.

But when you were the person sacrificing, you began to realize what that really meant. Now that DH-7 had put a million-dollar bounty on her head for anyone who killed her, she had a whole new perspective.

She raked a hand through her hair, trying to cast the thoughts aside as a smattering of wind and rain swooped down from the clouds and then disappeared.

She had to get back to lunch before everyone got suspicious.

As she started down the sidewalk, someone yelled, "On the left!" behind her.

Before Cassidy could move, a bike zoomed dangerously close beside her. She darted out of the way.

"Watch what you're doing!" Cassidy yelled after the biker.

He ignored her and kept going, earbuds preventing him from engaging with life around him—or taking any responsibility, apparently.

"Are you okay?" someone asked.

She looked up and realized a man, probably in his fifties, had caught her elbow as she'd jumped out of the way.

Cassidy straightened, her cheeks heating. "I'm so sorry."

"It's not your fault. That guy on the bike wasn't paying a bit of attention. Shame on him."

"You're right," Cassidy said. "He wasn't. I'm just glad no one was hurt."

As she took another step back, she saw three people gathered around the man. A woman—probably his wife. A teenage girl and a teenage boy. A family on vacation, most likely.

After she thanked him again, they turned to walk away. Something caught Cassidy's eye—a lightning tattoo behind the boy's ear.

A lightning tattoo that represented DH-7.

The boy turned to look at her, his gaze remaining on Cassidy.

Did he recognize her? Did he know about the bounty? Her role in disbanding the gang's leadership?

Cassidy sucked in a breath.

She needed to keep an eye on them because if there was one thing she'd learned from her time undercover, it was to trust no one.

CHAPTER
SIX

"EVERYTHING OKAY?" Ty's eyes searched Cassidy's as she returned to the table.

That was more than a bathroom break. She was breathless, her hair was slightly damp, and her cheeks flushed.

What happened?

Cassidy nodded, shoving a hair behind her ear and drawing in a shallow breath. "Everything's fine. I just ran into someone. I'm sorry for the delay."

"No problem," Del said. "We were listening to this guitar player. He's wonderful."

Another gust of wind blew over the area, almost taking away their napkins and possibly the entire table. Outdoor seating wasn't quite as glamourous on windy, storm-laden days.

"I think that's our cue to leave," Frank stood and placed some bills beneath a water glass. "Unless you're not finished eating, Cassidy."

Just as he said the words, a big fat plop of rain hit them.

"I'm finished," Cassidy said. "Thank you."

As Ty also stood, his phone buzzed. He scanned the screen and turned to Cassidy. "It's Mac. He wants to meet."

His mom stopped them mid-step and gave them her "don't argue with me" face. "Now, you two listen to me. I know we're here to visit, but I don't want you to put your life on hold. Your father and I can entertain ourselves. It would be nice if we could schedule some things together while we're in town, but I don't expect you to stop everything to be with us. We'll be just fine."

"Are you sure?" Ty asked, pulled between wanting to spend time with his parents and wanting to help Skye.

"Absolutely," Frank said. "Besides, I want to get some fishing in. I don't think that will happen until this storm passes, but I can head to the tackle shop. I also noticed a couple of your hurricane shutters are broken. I want to take a look at them."

"I read online that there's a flood watch right now," Del said. "So whatever you two are doing, be careful."

"We will." His mom would never stop mothering him, and Ty loved her for it. Most of the time, at least.

His parents dropped them both back at the house, and they hopped in Ty's truck then drove to meet Mac.

"So . . . what happened?" Ty asked. "Please don't say you got into a fight with the bathroom sink."

She told him about her potential Buddy sighting.

"You should have told me before you went after him," Ty said. "He could be dangerous."

Cassidy nibbled her lip. "I wasn't going to approach him. I just wanted to see if it was him. I didn't have time to think. Just to act."

"Do me a favor and tell me next time."

A strange look crossed through her gaze, but she nodded. "Okay."

Mac was waiting outside his house when they arrived, practicing drawing the gun from his holster, reminding Ty of a cowboy in a western flick. The man made life in Lantern Beach interesting.

"Oh, Mac." Cassidy chuckled.

"He lives for stuff like this," Ty said.

Cassidy nodded. "I can tell. He's a character."

"Everyone around here loved him as police chief. He has a way with people. He remembers their names and their stories, and he asks about the things they care about. There's a lot to be said for that."

"And then they elected Bozeman?"

"His dad is a state senator."

Cassidy's face tightened. What was up with that reaction?

Ty wasn't sure. He only knew that there was a lot about Cassidy he didn't know . . . and a lot she refused to talk about.

———

Cassidy leaned back, disturbed at the thought of Bozeman getting the job because of his dad. Yet, that new fact put some pieces in place. "Well, that explains it, I guess."

"Yeah, he has no idea what he's doing."

"That's a shame." Cassidy had been accused many times in her life of getting things because of her family connections. Usually, it wasn't justified. But in a way she felt a surprising touch of sympathy toward Bozeman.

Mac climbed in the passenger side, so Cassidy slid across the bench seat closer to Ty. A rush of self-consciousness flashed through her. She was close enough she could feel Ty's body heat. Smell his leathery cologne. Feel a prickle from the hair on his arm.

"Here we go! Let's go see what Bozoman missed." Mac let out a mischievous laugh and rubbed his hands together.

"Nice ride, by the way." Mac ran his hand across the shiny dashboard of Ty's truck.

Ty grinned. "Thanks. This girl was my sanity that first year after I was out of the military."

"I can imagine. Having a project to keep yourself occupied is always a good thing. You know I fought over in Vietnam, don't you?"

"No, I didn't realize that."

"I did. It was a hard time for our country, but the experience solidified for me that I wanted to be a cop."

"Why Lantern Beach?" Cassidy asked. "Did you ever think about some place larger or more exciting?"

He shrugged. "Nah. Not really. I wanted somewhere that felt like home, and this place fit the bill. There's enough drama and excitement in life without having to go out and look for it. Unless you consider that's what we're doing now. In that case, nix what I just said."

Cassidy mulled over his words. Could she ever be happy long-term in a place like this?

The thought seemed ludicrous. Her life was back in Seattle. Her family was there. It didn't matter that they weren't close. Her roots were three thousand miles across the country.

Ryan was there also, as was her job. A long line of

recruits would love to be a detective in Seattle. She'd worked hard to get the position.

She put those thoughts aside as Ty pulled up to the huge beachside house Buddy Macklemore had rented. They climbed out and stared at it for a minute before Mac dashed up the front steps and opened the door using a code he'd been given.

Inside was the typical vacation rental, decorated in pastels, with large windows showing expansive views of the ocean. Everything was designed for relaxation and peacefulness.

Except there was blood everywhere.

"Are you sure you're going to be okay seeing this?" Ty asked.

Cassidy snapped back to reality. Most people wouldn't be okay seeing a violent scene. Most people hadn't seen something like this uncountable times before.

She faked a shiver. "It's pretty gruesome."

He squeezed her arm. Which was sweet, but so unnecessary. She didn't let him know that.

It appeared there had been a fight here. A table was broken, and a shattered vase added a dangerous sparkle to the floor.

"I guess the police didn't clean up, huh?" Ty said.

"They don't," Mac said, seemingly unaffected by the scene. "It's not their job. The owner will have to either hire someone or do it themselves. A fact most people don't realize."

"I wouldn't want that job," Ty muttered.

"Most people don't," Cassidy said. "I mean, I imagine they wouldn't."

She'd met a few crime-scene cleaners in her day, and they were a special group of people.

"The police have probably already bagged any pertinent evidence," Mac said. "But knowing Bozoman, it's likely something was missed. Just watch your step."

Cassidy kept herself under control, desperate not to show her hand here. But this was what she did for a living. She examined crime scenes. Formulated an idea of what had happened. Marked evidence for later use at trial.

Something seemed off about this scene.

There were no drag marks coming from the pools of blood. No trickles leading to the door.

Why not?

There was, however, evidence of a struggle, of a fight. The blood pools weren't untouched, but they didn't show a logical progression of movement either. Someone bleeding out would have left a trail leading toward an exit.

What had happened to Buddy? Because there was no evidence that he'd left this place.

The thought didn't settle well with Cassidy.

She closed her eyes, picturing the scene. Maybe someone had shown up at Buddy's door. Perhaps Buddy had invited them over. It didn't matter. Either way, an argument had ensued—one that had led to a fight.

Assuming the blood was Buddy's, who would want to hurt the produce stand owner? He hadn't been in town long enough to develop enemies. Or had he? Was Skye an enemy?

"Hey, guys," Ty called from the other room. "Come look at this."

Cassidy and Mac met him in the kitchen.

A pad of paper rested beneath a landline phone, pencil marks slashed over the top.

Ty held up the top sheet. "I did that old trick I learned from Hardy Boy novels." He winked at Cassidy. "Not quite Sue Grafton, but . . . I decided to see what the last message left was. It's an address."

Oh, wasn't he funny?

"Brilliant work." Mac peered at the paper "That could be something important. Until we know for sure, let's keep looking. We don't want to raise suspicions by staying here too long, even if we do have permission."

Trying not to leave any evidence she'd been here—or fingerprints—Cassidy continued around the beach house. She climbed a set of stairs to the second floor, looking for Buddy's bedroom. Sure enough, his room was through the second door on the right at the top of the steps.

She wandered the perimeter of the room, soaking everything in.

For someone who'd set up a business in Lantern Beach, he certainly didn't appear to be staying long-term. He hadn't even unpacked his suitcase and instead appeared to be living out of it.

Which seemed odd.

Most people didn't come to town and set up a business temporarily. It wouldn't be worth it, especially considering the chunk of money he'd put into his top-of-the-line building.

Buddy could simply be too lazy to unpack. It wasn't unheard of. Or maybe he'd packed to go on a trip. But something told Cassidy that wasn't the case here.

Cassidy would also guess that renting this house cost

more per week than he made in a month. Another interesting fact.

Something wasn't adding up in her mind.

She flipped through some papers on the dresser. Pictures of produce. A list of what appeared to be sellers. No letters from Skye. Had Bozeman found them?

She didn't know. Just in case these proved handy, she took pictures of the list and the photos.

Just as she pulled open one of the dresser drawers, she heard a commotion downstairs.

She couldn't be sure, but it almost sounded like, "Police! Put your hands up."

Cassidy rushed toward the sound, slowing her steps as she neared the bottom of the stairs.

Ty and Mac stood there with their hands in the air, and Chief Bozeman had his gun aimed on them. The stout man already had beads of sweat on his upper lip and forehead. He was nervous. Really nervous.

"What do you think you're doing, Bozeman?" Mac asked, a toothpick dangling from his lips. He looked the opposite of the chief—as cool and composed as a man with a clear conscious.

"I'm responding to a breaking-and-entering call," he said. "What are you doing in here?"

A breaking-and-entering call? Who kept calling the police on this place?

Cassidy stopped at the base of the stairs and the chief pointed his gun at her also. "Hands up."

She complied, as any normal citizen might.

"We're here because Bill gave me permission to come inside," Mac said.

"Who's Bill?" Bozeman's eyebrows pinched together, and he drew his chin back in confusion.

"He owns this place." Mac said the words slowly, as if giving them a chance to sink into Bozeman's thick head.

The chief grunted. "Well, I didn't clear it."

"He told me that your officer said the scene was cleared."

"That didn't give you permission to come in here."

Mac didn't back down. "I think that was up to Bill."

Bozeman sighed and slid his gun back into the holster. "Put your hands down. But I reserve the right to arrest you."

"You have no grounds," Mac said.

If Cassidy didn't know better, she'd think Mac was enjoying this.

The chief narrowed his eyes. "What are you all really doing here?"

"We heard you were accusing a friend of ours of committing a crime you have no proof happened and no proof of her involvement in said crime," Mac said.

Cassidy let Mac take the lead here in order not to draw unnecessary attention to herself. Watching him was quite entertaining.

"We're exploring every aspect, but Skye Lavinia is at the top of our suspect list," Bozeman said. "She's got motive, means, and opportunity."

"Only if there's a crime," Mac said. "You can't prove anything. Maybe Buddy cut himself and drove himself to the mainland to see a doctor."

"Which is precisely why we haven't arrested her yet." Chief Bozeman raised his chin. "Now, I'd appreciate it if you'd leave, and I ask that you don't come back until I personally clear the scene."

Cassidy started to file out but paused beside the chief. "If you don't mind me asking, who reported we'd broken in?"

Again, there was no sign that they were up to anything nefarious. They'd had the code. It would make sense if they'd come in through a window or made a scene. But they hadn't.

"It was an anonymous tip," the chief said.

She nodded, not pushing anymore.

What exactly was going on here?

"And in case your friend didn't mention it," the chief continued. "She was covered in blood when we walked in."

CHAPTER
SEVEN
SIX WEEKS EARLIER

CADY PAUSED outside the door of the abandoned apartment building that DH-7 frequented. She tried to keep her anger at bay so she wouldn't blow her cover. But every fiber of her being wanted to demand answers until she knew the truth about what had happened after Raul had given her that drug.

Because that's what she realized had happened. She'd been drugged. It explained her memory lapse. Her headache. Her racing pulse.

And she knew exactly what they'd given her. Flakka— a drug that made people lose all their sensibilities.

She'd taken off the shirt she'd been wearing—the one covered in blood. The black tank top beneath it would hide any remaining stains. She'd then found a puddle of water in the warehouse—probably from a recent rainstorm. She'd done her best to remove all the red from her hands.

She couldn't walk down the street like that.

But her head still pounded uncontrollably, probably an

aftereffect of the drug and the shock she'd experienced once she'd come to.

She'd searched the warehouse before leaving. There were no dead bodies there, and no evidence that anything had happened.

Yet that blood had been fresh. It had still been wet. Still red. It hadn't darkened that much or deoxygenated—the process of blood turning brown as it met the air.

Drawing in another breath, she pulled the squeaky door open and stepped inside. The smell of cigarette smoke and body odor assaulted her. There was nothing good about this place.

A few people turned toward her, but most didn't give her much attention. Others were too busy counting their loves—money and drugs. Some were getting high. Others had circled up, probably discussing some kind of nefarious deed they were planning.

Cady needed to find Raul.

She'd broken into his inner circle surprisingly fast. Probably because she'd proven herself to be scrawny but strong. During that first initiation, someone had come at Raul. She'd stepped in and saved him.

Of course, it had all been a setup. Every step had been practiced and rehearsed. The man who'd come at Raul had been a cop, and he'd been okay—Cady had shot him with a rubber bullet.

But Raul had been impressed—impressed enough to trust her with assignments meeting his dealers. She hadn't let him down, even though everything in her had screamed that what she was doing was wrong.

She'd fought to get drugs off the street. To put killers behind bars.

And now she seemed to be supporting the very people she despised.

She just had to keep the end goal in mind. That was all she could do. All of this would pay off soon.

She reached the other end of the building—Raul's normal lair. The room was set up like a royal court, and Raul always sat enthroned on a leather chair against the center of the back wall—just like a king. Four guys surrounded him—his guard dogs, as Cady called them.

Raul's eyes lit with partial satisfaction, partial curiosity as he spotted her. "My Cady. You're back."

She glanced at the men around him, her stomach turning with revulsion at Raul's words. She wasn't his, and never would be. "Can I have a minute?"

His men moved closer, as if she might attempt a ruse against their leader.

"It's alright. This is my Cady. Of course we can talk. Just don't go too far."

They stepped out of the room, and Cady stepped closer. Even with all of her training, this man still scared the living daylights out of her. She'd never seen eyes so evil.

DH-7. Dead Haters Seven.

Because when the gang had first formed, seven members had tried to sell them out.

Each of those members had been strung up by their feet and left to bleed out in a deli one of the men owned.

That was what this gang did to people who betrayed them.

That person could be Cady if she wasn't careful.

"What can I do for you?" Raul asked.

Cady shoved down her nerves, refusing to show her

fear. "What happened?"

He smirked, knowing exactly what she was talking about. "What do you mean?"

"Don't play games with me, Raul. You gave me some flakka."

"I just couldn't understand why you didn't want to try it. It's like golden nectar from the gods themselves."

"I prefer to remain in control." Her voice trembled as she fought to do just that—remain in control.

His smirk grew wider. "And I wanted to see what you'd do if you weren't in control."

She swallowed hard. She didn't like the sound of that. Not at all.

What if she'd confessed to something under its influence? No, she couldn't have. She'd be dead now, if she'd done that.

"And what did I do?"

"You don't remember." He stood and came to stand face-to-face with Cady. He reached for her and traced a finger behind her ear.

She fought not to flinch or to turn away in repulsion. She knew what Raul thought of women—they were second class, a pleasure put on earth for men to enjoy and for nothing else.

She'd impressed him enough that he'd kept his distance. But for how long would that last?

"No, I don't remember." Her voice held a slight tremble still.

Which seemed to please Raul. He reached for her and pulled her closer until her body was shoved up against his. And then he leaned toward her neck, her ear. His lips didn't touch it, but his breath certainly did.

"You don't remember this?" he whispered, a menacing undertone lacing his voice.

Nausea roiled in her. What was he getting at? What had she done during those missing hours?

"I don't remember anything," she said, remaining steely in her determination to find answers.

He pulled back and laughed as if entertained by her response.

He stepped back. "We just officially made you one of us."

"What does that mean?" Part of her didn't want to know. Yet she had to know. Needed to know.

"We marked you."

The blood whooshed from Cady's lungs. Their tattoo. They must have given her a lightning bolt tattoo while she'd been under the influence.

"I see." She raised her chin. "But that still doesn't explain the blood or the warehouse. Did you just leave me?"

Raul backed away, done playing his games with her, obviously. "That's not important."

"It's important to me."

"The only thing that's important is that you understand that you're working for me." His gaze sliced into her. "Do you understand?"

She knew the conversation was over. "I understand."

"Good. Because I have another errand for you to run. Get cleaned up."

Cady bit down hard. This conversation might be over, but this ordeal was only just beginning for her. She would find answers about her missing time, if it was the last thing she did.

CHAPTER
EIGHT

CASSIDY AND TY sat beside each other in his truck, both quiet as they processed what they'd learned from Chief Bozeman at Buddy's house.

"I'm surprised Skye didn't mention she had blood on her hands," Ty said.

"She probably knew it would make her look guilty." Who wouldn't think that? Did it make it right not to mention it? Not really. Not to Cassidy, at least. Then again, Cassidy didn't have any room to talk, considering her current situation.

"But still." Ty shook his head, his jaw set and his eyes showing his unhappiness at the omission.

Cassidy shrugged. "Maybe she has a good explanation."

"Maybe."

Cassidy shivered. Hearing that her friend had blood on her brought back another round of memories. Every time she closed her eyes, she remembered her own situation.

And her internal cry was always the same. *Please, don't let me have hurt anyone while under the influence. Please.*

Who was she even talking to? Certainly not a God who'd been silent her entire life.

Or had He?

Her best friend, Lucy, had believed, and she'd been murdered. God certainly hadn't done her any favors.

"What now?" Ty said.

"Mac is going to get the information on the renter for us from Bill. In the meantime, how about if we go check out that address you used your Hardy Boy skills to find?"

"I was hoping you'd say that. I feel a little guilty not turning the information over to the chief."

Obstruction of justice—it was a crime. The process of living a lie had spilled over into so many other areas of her life. Things no longer seemed as black-and-white as they once had.

"I'm not sure the chief would buy our excuse," Cassidy said.

"Me neither." Ty put his truck into Drive. "Let's go."

Before he could pull out, something caught Cassidy's eye, and she grabbed Ty's arm. "Wait."

He hit the brakes. "What is it?"

"I just saw a man in that house over there." Cassidy pointed across the street. "He was watching us from his window."

"You think he's the guy who keeps calling in these tips?"

"I'd say it's a good possibility."

"Let's go find out."

He put the truck back into Park, and they dashed across the street, through the rain, to the man's house. The good news was that the weather had let up ever-so-slightly for the moment. There was only one car in the driveway, and the place seemed quiet—like it wasn't filled with a bustling family or partying friends.

Ty banged on the door, and they waited.

No answer.

They'd clearly just seen the man, however.

Ty pounded again.

And again, there was no answer.

Finally, Ty leaned toward the wood. "We know you're in there. Open up."

The door flew open, and a scrawny man stood there with his arms raised, a half-eaten plum in his hands. "Please, don't hurt me."

Ty scowled. "Why would we hurt you?"

"You were in that house." He nodded to Buddy's place.

Yep, he was the guy who kept calling the police.

"What's been going on in that house?" Cassidy asked. "And, please, put your hands down. We're not going to hurt you. We're just trying to figure out what's going on."

He eyeballed them both, searching their gazes to see if he could trust them. Finally, he nodded and stepped back. "I'll talk, but you need to come inside. I don't want anyone to see us."

Either this man was paranoid—which was a good possibility—or he knew something that could change this investigation.

They stepped into the entryway of the quiet home.

The man glanced outside again before shutting the door. Cassidy was thankful she'd thought to stuff her handgun into her cross-body purse. Just in case.

"Who are you two?" he asked, then took another bite

of the plum. The man had small features and dark hair that looked greasy. He wore exercise shorts and a T-shirt advertising a local restaurant.

"We're friends of someone accused of the crime," Ty said. "You mind sharing your name?"

"People call me Sissy." The man didn't even flinch at the name. When neither Ty nor Cassidy said anything, he explained. "My name is Sisco, but I got the name Sissy from my friends in college. It stuck, and now it sounds normal to me. Anyway, what can I do for you?"

"We know our friend didn't do it," Ty said.

"You mean the woman who broke in this morning?" the man said.

"She didn't break in," Cassidy said. "The door was unlocked—probably left that way by the real criminal."

"Well, she didn't belong there. That's why I called the police. I didn't want her to get hurt."

"How did you know she didn't belong there?" Cassidy asked.

"Because I've seen the type of people who frequented the place. They didn't look like that girl. They looked scary."

This was getting more interesting by the moment.

"So you called the police right after you saw her show up?" Cassidy asked.

"That's right. I didn't want the guilt of knowing she died because I did nothing."

Cassidy supposed that was noble enough.

"How much later did the police show up?" Ty asked.

"Probably five minutes."

So if the police had shown up five minutes after Skye arrived, Skye wouldn't have had time to kill Buddy and hide his body. Unless they'd thought she was there earlier as well.

"Are you here on vacation?" Cassidy needed to know more about this man's mental state.

Her partner had told her a story once about another cop who'd trusted a mentally unstable man who led the whole investigation on a wild goose chase. The real killer had almost gotten away. She'd never forgotten that warning.

"I am. Alone, which I know some people think is weird. But I prefer the quiet." He pushed his glasses up higher.

"Are you always so observant?" Cassidy continued, trying to figure the man out.

"I like to think so. I head up a neighborhood watch at my home in Raleigh. I work from home as a computer programmer, so I'm around to see a lot."

It seemed like someone would need to be kind of stable to do that job. Maybe this guy wasn't delusional.

"What about these other guys you saw go over there?" Cassidy said. "Could you tell us more about them?"

Sissy glanced at the window again, like he feared those men might reappear. "They looked scary. Like punks, if you know what I mean. And they came and went at weird hours."

"Did you see any of them this morning before our friend arrived?" Ty asked.

"I didn't, but I slept in today. It is vacation, after all."

"Thank you for your help," Ty said.

But Cassidy wasn't sure they were any further along than before.

———

Ty and Cassidy drove to the address they'd found at Buddy's house, only to discover it was an abandoned lot on the sound side of the island. There wasn't anything there except the trash someone had dumped in the tall grass and a no trespassing sign that Ty pulled to a stop in front of.

The rain had started coming down hard again, and it pounded against the roof of the truck. It also made visibility bad and painted a cloud of gray around everything in the area. The wind had picked up, and strong gusts occasionally rocked the vehicle.

"Why would Buddy have come here?" Cassidy asked, staring at the empty lot.

Ty showed her the paper with the address. "I'm not sure. Unless I'm not reading something correctly."

She studied the indention of the words against the gray pencil. "That's what it looks like to me. Maybe we just need to think this through a little more."

"Maybe we should." He glanced at his watch. "It's getting late anyway, so I should go home and check on my parents."

"You probably should."

His gaze caught hers. "Since we're dating this week, would you like to come?"

Cassidy felt the pull inside her. Part of her wanted to go and learn more about Ty. The other part of her wanted to obsess about this case—which would do her no good.

She decided she should go. "Of course I'd like to."

A grin spread across his face. "Great. But I'm warning

you—my parents can be over the top at times. I apologize in advance for anything they say."

"This is going to be fun." Cassidy's excitement shifted into a touch of dread then back to excitement.

Excitement because she wanted to learn more about Ty, but dread because of the ruse they were using. She finally settled with excitement. After all, she preferred figuring people out, and so far, Ty had been a tough nut to crack. Maybe his parents would give her more insight.

"Not over-the-top bad," he corrected. "Just over the top with their antics."

"I can see that."

His windshield wipers worked hard as sheets of rain came down.

"You don't talk about your parents very much," Ty said as they sloshed down the road.

His words caused Cassidy's heart to twist. Her cover story was that her dad was an engineer with his own firm in Texas and her mom was a homemaker. But the truth was that her dad owned a tech empire, easily making him one of the wealthiest men on the West Coast.

With that kind of success had come an unwavering dedication to his job. His conversations with Cassidy mainly consisted of him pushing her to do better than her best. Her mom had treated Cassidy like a little trophy she showed off to her friends instead of a daughter.

As an only child, she'd grown up feeling alone . . . except for her friend, Lucy. Then Lucy had been murdered, and that act had changed the course of Cassidy's life. No longer did she want to take over her father's business. No, she wanted to be a cop. She wanted to serve justice to those who felt as helpless as she did.

Her parents hadn't approved.

"We're not very close," Cassidy finally said. "I always felt like an outsider even among blood relatives. Even though I don't live near them anymore, I'm pretty sure it makes no difference in their lives."

"I'm sorry, Cassidy."

She shrugged, acting like it didn't bother her. "When you grow up with something like that, it feels normal. That is, until you see a family who acts like a family is supposed to act—warm and concerned for each other even with their differences. Then you realize what you've been missing out on."

"Sometimes when we see those things in our past, it makes us fight even harder to not be like that with our own families in the future. We learn from the mistakes of our parents."

"You sound like you know." Which was weird, since he appeared to have a close-knit family—one like Cassidy had always dreamed about.

"My family is a little too close sometimes. In a good way. But I saw my dad slave away at a factory job his entire life. He was an incredibly talented carpenter, but he never wanted to make the leap to doing it full-time. Now he's retired, but he has arthritis. I guess that taught me not to put my dreams on hold but to go for them. You just never know how much time you have."

"Exactly! That's why I became a—" Cassidy stopped herself. She'd almost said cop. "An interior designer."

"You feel passionate about it, huh?" Ty stole a glance at her.

She nodded, hating the lie. She couldn't care a lick

about paint colors or fabric swatches, but she'd pretend she did. "I love it."

"Maybe when I open my retreat center, you can help me put things together to make it relaxing and peaceful for the wounded warriors who visit."

She smiled at the thought of helping. It would be interesting trying to fake her skills in that scenario. "Yeah, maybe." She paused before adding in a teasing tone, "If we're still dating then."

Ty chuckled. "Good one."

She shrugged. "I thought so."

They pulled up to his house.

As they stepped outside, she glanced over toward her place. Cassidy's sedan was in the driveway, as well as Skye's old SUV and Elsa. The poor ice cream truck had been terribly neglected this week.

Most likely, Skye was upstairs. Cassidy would love to pepper her with more questions about what had happened. And to ask her about the blood that had been on her when police arrived.

But that would have to wait.

For now, she was going to hang out with Ty's family.

CHAPTER
NINE

WHEN THEY WALKED into Ty's place, his mom had prepared some sugar cookies, hot chocolate, and freshly popped popcorn. Rain pummeled the roof. Thunder rolled. Occasionally, a crack of lightning lit the sky.

"You know what tonight's the perfect evening for?" Del asked. "Game night!"

Cassidy smiled at the woman's enthusiasm. She was so different than her own demure, snobbish mom.

Halfway through a game of Apples to Apples, Ty's mom paused.

"Now you two," she said with a mischievous grin. "You don't have to pretend that you don't like each other around us."

Cassidy and Ty exchanged a glance.

"What do you mean?" Ty asked.

"I mean, it's like you're afraid to touch each other," she said. "I know you're probably just being cautious around here. But you two are young and in love. Nothing would make me happier than seeing the two of you act like it."

Cassidy's stomach sank. She did not want that.

"I'm not really big into PDA," Cassidy said, scooting away from Ty slightly.

Ty shook his head. "Me neither."

His mom gave him a look, and Cassidy knew there was more to that story.

"You two." Del shook her head. "I almost think you're hiding something."

Ty placed his hand on Cassidy's back, and tingles shot up her spine. "Just give us a while to get warmed up."

"Of course." His mom stood, casting one more grin their way. "Now, why don't we take a little break? I need to go make some more popcorn, and your father wants to help you fix that hurricane shutter. It's driving him batty because it keeps rattling against the house every time the wind blows."

Cassidy followed Del into the kitchen and began loading dishes into the dishwasher. Unfortunately, as Ty's "girlfriend" she should know how to get around the kitchen better. But she didn't, so she was going to do her best to fake it.

"You seem like a really nice girl, Cassidy," Del said, pouring kernels into a measuring cup. Kujo sat close by, waiting patiently for someone to drop a piece of food. "I've been praying for a long time that Ty would find someone like you. Especially after the mess with Renee."

At the mention of his ex-fiancée, Cassidy's pulse quickened. She'd been incredibly curious about what happened between the two of them. She shouldn't be. Their relationship was none of her business. But the bits and pieces she'd heard had made Cassidy's head spin.

"I know that was incredibly hard on him," Cassidy said, rinsing a plate.

His mom paused from her popcorn duty. "She was basically what kept Ty hopeful during those hard moments when he was working in the Middle East. He was stationed over there, unlike some SEAL teams. They were helping to train soldiers, as well as other things that he wasn't allowed to talk about."

"It's a noble—but difficult—calling."

"You can say that again." Del shook her head back and forth, a new somberness coming into her eyes. "He came back home, and she wasn't there to greet him. She'd moved back to Minnesota and had given his dog away."

"Not very admirable."

"Not at all." She leaned closer. "I never really liked her. She seemed flighty, you know? Like she was in love with the idea of being with a SEAL more than she understood just how difficult the profession was."

"At least he found out before they got married." Cassidy closed the dishwasher and looked for something else to distract herself with. She settled on giving Kujo a pat on the head.

"You're right. That is a good thing. I just wish it didn't hurt so much in the process, you know? Nothing's harder than seeing your kids suffer. You'll understand one day."

Except Cassidy probably wouldn't have kids. Ryan, the man she was truly dating, didn't want children. She'd convinced herself she was okay with that. But was she? She doubted it more and more every day.

She doubted her relationship with Ryan a little more every day, as well.

Did she want to marry someone who would give her

the same life she'd grown up with? She'd end up following in her parents' footsteps. But, on a logical level, she and Ryan made sense together. Could there be more to marriage than logic?

The answer seemed like a no-brainer now that she'd removed herself from the situation.

Or was it because she'd been around Ty and seen a different kind of life? A simpler life away from the pressures of money and status and people in power.

"Then there was Goldman," his mom continued, shaking the pot on the stove as kernels began popping.

Cassidy straightened. Goldman? Who was he? Ty had never mentioned the name, but Cassidy felt certain she should act like he had—if she wanted to keep her cover.

"He doesn't like to talk about him." Cassidy shoved her hip against the counter, giving up on making herself useful.

"Oh, no. Of course not. Everything changed after Goldman died, though. Everything."

Before Cassidy could ask any more questions, Ty and his dad walked in from outside.

But now Cassidy was more curious than ever.

———

Ty walked Cassidy home, his steps slow and unhurried, despite the rain.

He'd had a surprisingly good time tonight with her. She fit in with his family in a way that amazed even him. Maybe Cassidy coming to this area and moving in beside him was all a part of a bigger plan.

No, he corrected himself. He couldn't let his thoughts

go there. He had a mission while here in Lantern Beach. He was trying to start a nonprofit for wounded war veterans. He was still trying to raise the capital he needed, but it was slow going. He wasn't a business type of guy. No, he was a former soldier. But he was determined to make this happen.

Right now, his main mission was helping Skye.

"Your parents are really great, Ty," Cassidy said, slowly climbing the steps to her place.

"Yeah, they are, aren't they?"

"And they seem so happy. How long have they been married?"

"Thirty-five years."

"That's awesome. I wonder what their secret is."

He shrugged, shoving his hands into his pockets. "My dad told me once that you needed to marry a friend you could flirt with."

Cassidy smiled. "I like that."

"Yeah, I do too." Though there was a lot to be said for the wild feelings and emotions that came with romance, in the end it boiled down to having someone at your side whom you liked. Whom you had fun with. Who shared your principles and values.

He thought he'd had that with Renee, but, looking back, the two of them had just been different. Too different. He just hadn't seen it at the time.

As they reached Cassidy's door, he paused. He felt like there was something he needed to say—he just didn't know what.

He glanced at Cassidy, at how lovely she looked as she stood there with that gentle smile on her face.

He opened his mouth, not sure what was about to

come out. Before any words could leave his lips, his phone rang. He glanced at the screen before holding up the phone.

"It's a call from a friend on the West Coast," he said. "I need to take this."

Cassidy's face looked a little paler. Why was that?

"I'll talk to you later," Cassidy said.

He nodded, waved goodbye, and then answered, anxious to hear what his friend had to say.

———

Back at Cassidy's house, Skye was already in bed and had left a note that read, "I'm exhausted. Sorry to head to bed so early. We'll talk in the morning."

And they would have plenty to talk about tomorrow. But for now, Cassidy was almost glad her temporary guest was asleep. She needed some time by herself.

Ty had gotten a call from the West Coast? Surely that was a coincidence. The West Coast was a big place, and there was no reason to believe that a call like that would have anything to do with Cassidy. Yet, a part of her felt unsettled—and possibly paranoid—at the thought.

She could trust Ty, right?

She let out a breath. She honestly didn't know whom she could trust—not with a million-dollar bounty on her head. People would go to desperate lengths for that amount of money, and that was one more reason why no one could know Cassidy's true identity.

Shoving those thoughts aside, Cassidy hopped on her computer and started her search. Her normal search. The one she'd done hundreds of times already.

She scoured news articles for anything about a murder or dead body that might be connected to the day she'd woken up covered in blood.

Foolishly perhaps, she hadn't mentioned the incident to anyone.

Maybe she should have. But she'd known how it would look. She might go to jail—all for a crime she couldn't remember. She wanted to investigate for herself first.

So that's what she'd been doing. Investigating herself.

She'd narrowed her possibilities into a short list. She didn't dare write them down. Instead, she stored the information in her head.

Most of them were cases with fuzzy details. She checked daily to see if there were any updated news articles on them.

Cassidy needed to know if she'd done something horrible while she'd been undercover.

If she had . . . she didn't know how she'd live with herself. Her family would probably turn their backs on her. So would all her colleagues on the police force. She wouldn't blame them.

And everyone knew what happened to cops in prison . . . not to mention the fact she'd be with the members of DH-7 that she'd put away.

She'd be a dead woman walking.

Yet if she'd done something horrible, she needed to do the time. She just wanted something more concrete before she opened up that door. She wanted to go to trial first and put those gang leaders away.

She shoved those thoughts aside as she began her usual research.

She checked each victim's name, running it through a search engine. She reminded herself to clear the browser from any cache and cookies since it could potentially lead someone back to her.

The first two victims didn't have any new information.

But the third one did.

She held her breath as she read the updated article.

"Sandra Connors's body was found on May 5 in a remote alley in Seattle. The medical examiner's report indicated that she had been bludgeoned to death. The police still have no new leads, though they suspect involvement with DH-7 due to a lightning mark left on the victim."

Nausea roiled in Cassidy's stomach. Bludgeoned to death? DH-7?

She flipped to another screen and stared at the woman's picture. Sandra had been forty years old with blonde hair cut in a style that made her appear older. She had a round face but a great smile. She wasn't married and had no kids, though she had been dating a man named Jim Levinson.

The first time Cassidy had seen her picture, there'd been no flash of recognition. But now she'd stared at it so much that the woman did seem familiar. Her thoughts and emotions tangled with each other until she didn't know which to trust. Could she seem familiar because her subconscious knew they'd met before? Or was it simply the act of staring so often at the woman's picture that had made her seem familiar?

On a whim, she dug out her burner phone—the one that only two people had the number for. She called Samuel

Stephens, the task force leader and an FBI agent. He was the one who'd approached Cassidy about taking part—an undercover part—in the investigation. Apparently, they'd thought, out of all the officers they had to pick from, that she could best blend in with the DH-7. It was strange considering she'd grown up privileged, but she supposed her age and size and singleness had played a factor.

"Cassidy," he answered. "Funny you called because I was going to call you. What's going on?"

"I need a favor," Cassidy started, leaning back in the stiff wooden desk chair. "Could you look into the murder of a woman named Sandra Connors? See if you can find out any details about her death?"

He paused for a minute. "Anything I should know?"

"No, not really." Cassidy drew in a deep breath. "I just need information, but I prefer not to discuss specifics until I know more."

"I'll see what I can find out for you then."

Cassidy released her breath. Good. That was done, and maybe he'd find out something that could help her. Maybe he could direct her. Because it was becoming harder and harder to live with her questions and to contend with the unknown.

"You said you had something to discuss." Cassidy straightened, her gut telling her his news wasn't good.

"I do." His voice grew grim. "A woman was murdered down in San Diego."

She knew there was more to this because a murder in California wasn't all that uncommon. So she waited for him to continue.

"The woman was shot multiple times in a parking lot.

Based on the streak of lightning left on her forearm, DH-7 is responsible."

"I'm sorry to hear that."

"I don't think you understand, Cassidy." Samuel's voice crackled over the line. "We believe that gang members thought this woman was you."

All the blood drained from Cassidy's face so quickly that her head began to spin. "Say that again."

"The woman looked like you," Samuel said. "She had the same petite, thin frame. She had long, dark hair that she'd pulled back into a bun—just like you used to wear yours. The same facial structure. From a distance, we believe these gang members thought they'd found you."

Cassidy lowered her head against the desk, afraid she might pass out. The woman sounded like the old Cassidy —before she'd colored her hair and let it go wavy. "I . . . I don't know what to say."

"There's nothing you can say, Cassidy," Samuel said. "There's nothing you can do."

"But me being in hiding is putting innocent people at risk! I can't let that happen." Nausea roiled in her gut.

"If you don't, then more people will die. We need your testimony to put these guys away permanently. That's the bigger picture . . ."

"But—"

"There are no buts. I was hesitant to tell you, but knew you'd want to know. I thought you could handle this news as well. You've got mental stamina, which was one of the reasons we chose you to go undercover in the first place."

Her throat clenched. Samuel was right. Cassidy knew he was. But it didn't make her feel any better.

"Certainly they realized the woman wasn't me," she finally said, her tone dull with each word.

"We can only assume that, just like we can only assume they're still out there looking for you."

Time seemed to freeze around her at the thought.

"Does Ryan—Mr. Samson—know?" she asked. No one knew about her relationship with Ryan, and they wouldn't know until after the upcoming election.

Ryan said Cassidy's father was a polarizing figure, and he didn't want anything to hinder his chances of being elected as the prosecuting attorney.

"Of course he knows," Samuel said. "As the attorney on the case, he was one of the first people we spoke with."

Ryan knew? And he hadn't told her? Granted, he was only supposed to call in an emergency. But Cassidy would consider that news worthy of an emergency.

"You going to be okay?" Samuel asked.

Cassidy clamped her eyes shut. "Yeah, I'm fine."

"Just keep doing what you're doing. Lie low. I know it's hard for a type A gal like you, but the end result is going to be worth it."

She ended the call and quickly hid the phone in a secret compartment at the bottom of her purse. Then she leaned back in her chair, her head spinning.

On a logical level, she knew what Samuel said was true. But just the thought of other people suffering because of her . . . she couldn't stomach it.

It's difficult to wait, but more difficult to regret.

She had to remember the big picture. But that was becoming harder and harder every day.

CHAPTER
TEN

TODAY'S GOALS: FIND MORE
ANSWERS—ABOUT EVERYTHING.

SKYE WAS ALREADY UP and sitting at the kitchen
table the next morning when Cassidy emerged.

Cassidy had heard her guest clunking around the
house. Being aware was what Cassidy was trained to do—
to listen, to observe, to formulate. Besides, she hadn't been
able to sleep.

Cassidy had stayed in bed an extra hour, but not
because she was sleeping. No, she just needed more time
alone to wrestle with her thoughts. To contend with her
guilt even more. To wonder why it felt like things were
just getting worse and worse.

Finally, she'd gotten dressed and joined Skye, trying to
forget about her own problems in order to listen to her
friend's. Because one look at Skye's face, and Cassidy
knew the woman was having a rough time.

"Did you get any sleep?" Cassidy slipped her hands
around a cheerful yellow coffee mug as she lowered
herself across from Skye.

"Not much. I kept halfway expecting the police to

show up in the middle of the night to arrest me." Skye absently flicked her hair out of her face, revealing red-rimmed eyes that shifted, not making contact.

"The good news is that the police don't know you're here," Cassidy offered. "At least, they shouldn't know. I certainly didn't tell them."

"That's true."

Cassidy rubbed the side of her ceramic mug, contemplating her next question. She hoped she could ask it with compassion. "Skye, Chief Bozeman said there was blood on you when he arrived at the house yesterday. You . . . you didn't mention that."

Skye's head dipped down, and she squeezed the skin between her eyes. "I know. I'm so sorry. I knew how it would sound, though."

Why did suspects—even innocent ones—always leave out suspicious details? Didn't they realize it made them seem guiltier? "What happened?"

Skye raised her head, but her eyes were rimmed with tears and her face looked pale—to a worrisome extent. "When I got to Buddy's house, the door was unlocked. That was the truth. I shoved it opened, but it was a little stuck. So instead of stepping inside, I fell inside. And I fell right into that pool of blood." Her voice broke as a cry escaped. "It was horrible."

"I can imagine. Did the police seem to buy that story?"

"Buy it? You think someone has to buy it?" Her eyes widened with fear.

Cassidy quickly back tracked. "I understand what you're saying, Skye. But it's the police's job to dig deep and to not accept people's word without proof. I'm just wondering how they reacted."

That seemed to calm Skye. Her shoulders slumped ever so slightly, her tension visibly dissolving a touch. "I mean, they let me go but told me to stay in town."

"As you were sleeping last night, did you think of anything else that might be pertinent to the investigation?" It was amazing what sleep could do sometimes. Cassidy had had many realizations after getting some shut-eye.

Skye twisted her lips, half-nibbling on one. "I was thinking about Buddy's produce stand. He was getting a higher class of clientele than me for some reason."

"What do you mean?"

"I mean, there were a lot of nice cars pulling up to his place when compared with mine."

"Could that be because his looked newer and—" How did Cassidy say it?

"Nicer?" Skye finished.

Cassidy shrugged, hoping she hadn't hurt her friend's feelings. "Yours just looks more whimsical. Besides, you said vacationers and out-of-towners frequented his place. People coming here have a tendency to have more money than locals, so price isn't really a sticking point for them."

She nodded, seeming happy with Cassidy's assessment. "Yes, that's what I figured also. But something about the whole setup just seems fishy to me."

"I agree."

"Are you going to keep investigating today?"

Cassidy glanced out the window at the torrents of rain falling from the sky. "Yes. I don't think I'll be selling any ice cream again today."

"Thank you. I can't tell you how much this means to me."

"It's no problem, Skye. I'd want someone to do it for me."

Samuel *was* doing it for Cassidy. He just didn't know it yet.

———

Cassidy should probably handle the rest of this investigation alone. It was better if she continued to put distance between herself and Ty. This week she'd have to compromise on that some—after all, they were "dating" temporarily. But she didn't have to go overboard.

As soon as she reached her driveway, Ty appeared from his downstairs shed, Kujo on his heels.

Her throat clenched as she soaked in Ty's freshly showered appearance. His hair was still damp and spiky. She itched to reach up and feel his unshaven cheek.

Why did this man have this effect on her? She didn't even like him. He was kind of cocky, he didn't care what people thought of him, and he liked to aggravate her. What was there to like about that?

Thunder rumbled overhead, and Cassidy was thankful her driveway was beneath her house because a shower of rain poured from the sky at that moment. She leaned down and greeted Kujo with a nice long rub on his head. The dog showed his appreciation by leaning into her.

"I was hoping I'd catch you," he said. "I didn't want to call because I thought you might be sleeping. How's Skye?"

She shifted her keys from one hand to the other. "She's hanging in. About as well as can be expected, I guess."

"Is she upstairs alone?"

"Lisa is coming over for a while. Skye insisted I get out and look for answers. At this point, I think she'd take anyone digging for answers and being on her side."

"So what's our plan?" he asked.

Cassidy bit back a frown. While part of her was delighted at the prospect of working with Ty, the other part reminded her that it was best not to get too close. But if she feigned an excuse right now, he'd probably only get suspicious.

"I thought it would be a good idea to check out the produce stand," she said, remaining noncommittal about working with Ty.

"Why's that?"

Cassidy shrugged, trying to downplay her thoughts for the sake of not looking professional. She was becoming pretty good at it. "Skye said Buddy always got a higher class of clientele. There's probably going to be nothing there, but I just want to check it out for myself."

"Sounds good. Let's go." He nodded toward his truck.

"You want to drive?" He *always* wanted to drive. And she hadn't even asked him to help her.

"Why not? I guess I'm old-fashioned like that."

Old-fashioned? Cassidy had to admit that an old-fashioned type of guy had never had much appeal to her. No, she liked modern guys who respected women as equals. Who liked to vacuum and do dishes.

But something about hearing Ty say it was appealing. Probably because Ty was the type who would be chivalrous while still helping around the house. He was balanced, and Cassidy found that fascinating.

Ryan let her have her independence, so much so that it almost felt like he didn't care at times.

No, that was a crazy thought. Of *course* Ryan cared.

But maybe the thought wasn't so crazy. Not if Cassidy listened to the nagging doubts plaguing her lately.

Ty paused at the edge of the shelter, right on the dry side of the driving rain. "If you really want to, you're welcome to drive."

He stared at her—almost leaned toward her—as he waited for her response.

Cassidy opened her mouth, about to agree. Before she could say anything, Elsa—the ice cream truck—began singing "Who Built the Ark?" How appropriate, considering if this rain kept coming, they might need an ark.

She wandered toward Elsa and played with the knobs there. Some kind of short circuit made the music play at random times. The anomaly kept life . . . interesting.

She turned back to Ty, torn between working with him or going solo. "If you go with me, I suppose you can drive. But only because your truck is awesome."

"I'll address the 'if you go with me' part later. Right now, I just want to document that you said my truck is awesome."

She crossed her arms. "I've always liked your truck. I didn't like your cousin's truck with all of his naughty bumper stickers."

"Naughty?"

"You have to admit . . ."

"Yeah, they were pretty bad."

"And I have to admit that a truck like your real one can even make someone like you look good." Her eyes glimmered with teasing.

There she went again. She'd never been a teaser. But something about Ty brought it out in her.

Was she . . . flirting?

No, that couldn't be it.

He stepped closer, a smile tugging at his lips and his own sparkling eyes reflecting hers. "Is that right?"

She kept her chin high. "Yeah, that's right."

"You're . . ." He shook his head and stepped back.

What? What was he going to say? "I'm what?"

He paused and turned back toward her. "You're unlike any woman I've ever met."

She didn't bother to ask if that was a good or bad thing. Instead, she'd take it for a compliment. "You know, on second thought, I should go alone."

"You're not going alone."

"But you need to spend time with your family."

He froze then released a breath and shook his head. "You're unbelievable."

"What's that mean?"

"It means this." He scooped down and threw Cassidy over his shoulder, despite her protests.

She pounded on his back. She could totally take him out if she wanted—but it would blow her cover.

"What are you doing?" she shrieked.

"I can't let you go out there alone."

"Of course you can. I'm a professional—" She stopped cold.

"A professional ice cream lady? Interior designer?"

Detective, she wanted to scream. But she couldn't.

"I'd feel horrible if something happened to you." Ty darted through the rain toward his place. "I can't put you in danger."

She bit her tongue. "I'll be fine."

"Yes, you will—because I'm going with you." He

opened his truck door and plopped her in the passenger seat. Then he leaned in, as if she might try to escape.

Cassidy sucked in a deep breath at his closeness, at his presence, at his broad form.

"Oh, look at you two!" someone exclaimed. "You finally look like you're dating. I just had to catch you at the right moment."

Del stood there, grinning from ear to ear.

Cassidy leaned back, knowing she wouldn't be able to do this solo, no matter what she tried.

———

Ty couldn't help but grin as they headed down the road. Cassidy was truly unlike anyone he'd met before. She was confident and funny, and she knew how to handle herself in tense situations.

He liked that.

Don't like it too much, he reminded himself.

As tempting as the idea was, the last thing he needed was another woman in his life. Things were so much simpler when he was single. He could do his own thing. Work on the retreat center he wanted to start. Wrestle with his own demons without getting anyone else involved.

No, women just made life more complicated, especially when they broke your heart.

The rain came down in buckets. A report came on his radio as they sloshed down the road, advising of a possible flood warning on the island.

He'd been around here enough to know that flood warnings weren't to be taken lightly. He'd witnessed entire houses wiped out by rising waters. He'd seen streets destroyed and vehicles swept away.

It was one of the dangers of living on an island that some geologists believed was sinking as sea levels rose. Eroding shorelines only added to the dangers. Yet he wouldn't trade this place for the world. Lantern Beach was a slice of paradise.

He stole a glance at Cassidy. She stared out the window, her mind seeming to be in another place.

She got like that a lot.

What was she thinking? Exactly what did she leave behind to come here?

She was never quick to talk about her past, though Ty knew a few details. There was still a lot of mystery surrounding the woman—and it was a mystery he itched to crack.

But if Cassidy knew that, no doubt she would freak out. Most women wouldn't approve of him using his Navy SEAL training to track down information about them.

No, he'd find out the traditional way.

"Did you have a good talk with your friend last night?" Cassidy asked, but her voice sounded almost raw.

"My friend?"

She glanced at him. "From the West Coast?'

"Oh, yeah. Steve. He's in San Diego."

Her face went white again. What a strange reaction.

"He's a SEAL," he told her. "He's stationed out there."

She released a breath and nodded. "Of course."

"But, yeah, he's doing well. Hoping to come out here soon for a visit."

A few minutes later, he pulled into the gravel parking by Skye's produce stand.

Cassidy gave him a look.

"I figured it was less obvious to park across the street, just to be safe," he explained.

"Good choice."

Ty paused before getting out, knowing he'd get drenched, even with the short run from his truck to the shopping area covered by a quaint tin roof.

Skye's stand, on the other hand, was all handmade and salvage-store purchased. An old turquoise van with one side removed and replaced with a wooden pergola with peeling brown paint. Her baskets displaying the fruits and vegetables were all mismatched. Handwritten signs displayed the prices and were blown away on windy days. Yet all the produce was local, even if it had some bruises or less-than-desirable shapes and sizes.

"This place is surprisingly nice." Cassidy ducked for a better look at Buddy's place of business. She'd only get glimpses through the pouring rain, but they'd both seen enough to realize that.

"Someone said this place was brought in on a tractor trailer. It was already together and just had to be set up. And, I never mentioned this to Skye, but apparently the man even sold peach . . . well, peach everything. Ice cream, shakes, slushes, tea. I heard it was really good, but out of loyalty's sake, I never tried any."

"Loyalty's a good trait to have," she said.

"Well, at least you think there's one good thing about me." Was he fishing for a compliment? Quite possibly— and there was no shame in that.

She cast him a wry smile. "At least."

And Cassidy wasn't taking the bait. Just one more thing to admire about her.

"Let's go!" she said, opening her door.

The sound of the rain intensified, and a coolness swept through the truck.

The temperature was dropping, which meant—

Another rumble of thunder seized the air, reminding them that this domain belonged to nature—and to God. It was never a bad thing to be put in place and reminded how small you were in the grand scheme of things.

He darted out after Cassidy and paused below the awning, shaking his head to rid his skin and hair of the raindrops.

Cassidy shrieked good-naturedly and held her hands up as another round of moisture hit her. "Really?"

As Ty glanced at her, his breath caught. Her hair clung to her face, and her form-fitting jean shorts and T-shirt also hugged her body a little tighter. Cassidy nibbled on her bottom lip as her eyes clearly indicated she was feeling playful.

Ty had the craziest urge to step closer and—

"Let's get started," Cassidy said, turning away from him.

Right. They'd come here to do something. Why was Ty letting himself get distracted like this?

He turned to focus on the task at hand, his pulse still pounding. And this was why he'd thought having female Navy SEALs was a bad idea. Men were way too easily distracted. Enough said.

"Well, this is a fruit and vegetable stand," she started, staring at the assortment of veggies in front of her. "Interesting that Buddy left out all of this produce. Wouldn't you think he'd be afraid someone would steal it? I think Skye takes her produce in every night."

Ty nodded behind him. "There is an indoor area that he keeps locked up. But I guess he thought it wasn't worth the hassle of bringing everything in every night."

"Brave man."

"Or stupid."

"True that." She picked up a tomato—a perfect looking tomato—and examined it. "This is from a greenhouse. No homegrown tomato I've ever bought looks this good."

"I have to agree."

Cassidy began pacing, still gripping that tomato. "So is the produce stand connected with his disappearance?"

"Your guess is as good as mine," Ty said. "Everything appears normal here."

She walked over toward the door and jiggled it. It was locked. Of course.

"You know how to pick a lock?" Cassidy asked, stealing a glance at Ty.

His eyes widened. "You want me to break in?"

"Not really break in." She shrugged. "Just pick the lock."

He chuckled and shook his head. "That would be breaking in."

"I know, but breaking in sounds so much more criminal."

"Because it is," Ty said.

"Maybe I can do it." She put the tomato down and pulled something from her hair. "How hard can it be? They make it look so easy on TV."

"And in those crime novels you've been reading?"

She exaggerated her agreement with an emphatic nod.

"Exactly. According to those novels, anyone can be a detective."

Ty smiled. He was going to let Cassidy try. And when she discovered she couldn't, they'd leave, and no one would be in trouble.

"Got it!" Cassidy turned toward him, a wide smile on her face.

Surprise flashed through Ty. "You got what?"

Certainly he wasn't understanding something.

Cassidy gave the door a shove, and it opened, revealing boxes inside. "I got the door open."

"How'd you do that?" He had the strange desire to scratch his head in confusion.

"I told you it wasn't that hard. Because everything you see on TV *is* apparently true."

"You're something else." He let out another chuckle. Yet one more way this woman had surprised him. Cassidy could pick locks. It had to be a fluke because picking locks wasn't that easy.

Cassidy cast him another smile and stepped inside, a rebellious side of her emerging. "Come on."

Ty looked around but didn't see anyone. And this was the perfect time to be here because the pouring rain offered perfect cover.

Yet the law-abiding side of him hesitated.

Skye. This was for Skye.

After a moment of hesitation, he stepped inside. The place was filled with more produce, most of it in boxes. There was also an ice cream machine and all the fixings for Buddy's peach concoctions.

Cassidy opened one of the boxes and held up a cantaloupe. "Ah ha! Look at this."

She turned the fruit around and showed him a sticker on the other side—a sticker that proved this stand wasn't selling local fruit and veggies.

"You really think he died because his produce wasn't homegrown?" Ty stepped closer and took the cantaloupe to examine it.

"Not necessarily. But it seems like something we should keep in mind."

He held up a roll of stickers from the counter and squinted. "Even stranger, here are brand new stickers. He was placing them on the produce himself."

Cassidy paused and jutted a hip out. "Why would he do that?"

"That's a great question."

Cassidy pulled out her phone and snapped a few pictures.

Before they could talk anymore, a car pulled into the parking lot, the rumble of tires barely audible over the rain. Cassidy jerked her head toward Ty. He'd heard it too.

Normally he liked to own up to what he was doing. But his gut told him, in this situation, they needed to hide.

Because this was about more than homegrown produce.

CHAPTER
ELEVEN

CASSIDY'S HEART pounded in her ears as Ty jerked her behind the counter.

"Under there," he whispered.

She halfway wanted to confront whoever had shown up. But what if it was the chief again? How were they going to explain to Bozeman that they were interfering yet again in his investigation? It wouldn't look good.

She squeezed beneath the counter, ignoring what could be the remains of pureed peaches and any critters that might have been feeding on them. Mainly ants.

Ty reached beneath a wall panel and jerked something. The lights went out. Thankfully, this place hadn't been constructed as a permanent structure, which made cutting the electricity that much easier.

He slid beneath the counter with her just as footsteps vibrated across the wooden floor of the shed.

Whoever was here was inside. Probably a man based on the heavy thud of the footsteps. The intruder was taking it slowly, as if assessing the stand.

Cassidy desperately wanted a glimpse of him, wanted to see who was here. But she didn't dare move. Not until she knew more.

And Ty's instincts seemed reliable as well. If both of them thought this could be trouble, then they needed to be wise.

As they waited and listened, and as each moment seemed to slow to a thick gel, Cassidy became keenly aware of Ty behind her. She could feel his heartbeat against her back. Could feel him breathing against her neck and hair. Could smell that tantalizing leather aftershave.

But it was more than that. His presence also brought Cassidy a weird sense of comfort. The man was strong and capable and smart. And—

Before her thoughts could go any further, the footsteps drew closer.

The visitor was probably only a foot away. Cassidy turned her head—though barely. But from the corner of her eyes she spotted legs. Whoever was here wore jeans and some expensive-looking loafers.

Why had someone come by? It was almost as if he'd been alerted there was something going on here and had come to check it out.

This wasn't the police chief, however. The clothes and shoes were too expensive.

Could it be Buddy? What if he wasn't dead? What if he was just in hiding?

Cassidy could feel Ty's heartbeat increase against her back. His adrenaline was pumping also, wasn't it? He was preparing for the worst.

Her phone, she realized. Had she left it on the counter

after she took that picture?

She was usually more careful than that. But Ty had grabbed her so quickly and pushed her under here, she'd barely had time to think. Or maybe her skillset was slipping since she hadn't been able to put her investigative talent to use.

Whatever the reason, this wasn't good.

The intruder paced closer. Flipped through something on the countertop above them. Let out a grunt.

And then he left. But neither Cassidy nor Ty dared to move. They had to know he was gone first.

Finally, they heard an engine start. Tires on the gravel.

And they knew the man was gone.

Cassidy let out her breath. That had been close.

And now she needed to see about her phone.

Ty climbed out, stretching his long legs. A second later, he bent down and offered his hand. "The coast is clear. Come on out."

Cassidy let him help her out. But as soon as she stood, her eyes went to the counter and her stomach dropped.

"We have a problem, Ty," she said. "Whoever was here . . . he took my phone. That means he very well could figure out who I am."

———

Ty called Skye and asked her if she wanted to meet at the Crazy Chefette for lunch. Skye agreed, and Ty and Cassidy took off down the road. Rain continued to come down by the bucketful. But Cassidy hardly noticed. She was too busy thinking about her phone.

"Did you have personal information on your home screen?" Ty asked.

Cassidy let out a sigh. "No, I have a sunrise picture—nothing that would specifically identify me."

"That's good news."

"I suppose. I just can't believe I made that mistake." How could she have been so stupid?

"Why would you think about it otherwise?" Ty said. "It's not like you've done this before."

If only he knew . . .

"I wonder who that guy was," Cassidy said, changing the subject before she gave anything away.

"I couldn't tell much about him, other than he had expensive tastes. Those weren't cheap shoes he was wearing."

"I noticed that also. I wonder if it was Buddy. I mean, I did think I saw him yesterday."

"That was a lot of blood for someone to lose and still be walking around."

She shrugged. "Well, it wasn't the police chief. At least he didn't catch us again."

"Both of us could be off base. Maybe it was someone who wanted to buy some apples and was checking to see if the place was open."

Cassidy was pretty sure Ty didn't even believe his own words. He was just trying to make her feel better.

They pulled up to Lisa's restaurant, the Crazy Chefette. As they walked in, the scent of garlic and cinnamon hit them. The place was surprisingly empty. The rain must have kept some of the crowds at home today.

Ty and Cassidy found a corner table and grabbed it

while they waited for Skye. They ordered glasses of water to hold them over until their friend showed up.

Cassidy glanced behind her and saw Mac sitting at the counter area—his usual place—talking to his friends and telling his stories. The man liked to have an audience, and he always seemed to find one here.

When he spotted them, he wandered their way and slid in beside Cassidy.

"Anything new?" Mac asked, volleying his gaze between the two of them.

"Not really," Ty said. "Just dead-ends. You?"

"My friend got back to me with the information on the man renting the house," he said. "But I already ran a check on him. Buddy Macklemore doesn't exist—not legally, at least. His name is fake, and so is his home address and social security number even. So that lead didn't get us anywhere."

"Good to know," Cassidy said.

"The scanners were abuzz this morning with some kind of update that the chief had to rush back to the station to hear about."

"What was it?" Ty asked.

"They didn't say, and I haven't been able to get it out of anyone. I also talked to Bower Wilson, the man who told Skye about Buddy's spy."

Cassidy perked. "Did he say anything?"

"No, just that apparently *he* was the spy," Mac said. "Buddy gave him a whole basket of free fruit and vegetables for the information. It seemed like a shady business practice, but nothing that would indicate trouble."

Cassidy's gaze crossed the restaurant. One of the

Lantern Beach police officers had just come in and taken a seat on the other side of the dining area.

"Maybe you can get some information from him," she muttered.

Mac pointed to himself. "Me? No, he won't tell me anything. But he might talk to you."

"What do you mean?" Cassidy asked.

"He loves pretty blondes, and he's known to have loose lips. You should give it a try."

"I'd hate myself if I did," she muttered. Not that she was above it. She'd used her new blonde status to butter up people in the past, but she never liked herself much afterward.

"You're our best hope," Ty said.

She did a double take, surprised that Mr. Always-Virtu-ous-Except-When-It-Came-to-His-Family wanted to go along with this. "I thought for sure you'd disapprove of those methods."

"One thing I learned as a SEAL was that, in battle, you have to identify weaknesses in your enemy's defense. I'm not saying Officer Quinton is an enemy. But I am saying he's a weakness. And a weak spot is always the first place you look when breaching."

Cassidy kind of liked the Navy SEAL talk. She'd worked with a lot of tough guys, but there was something about Ty that was different—more rugged and confident.

With a sigh, she stood. "I'll do it. But I don't have any hopes that this will work."

CHAPTER
TWELVE

CASSIDY STOOD, straightened her outfit, and threw her blonde hair over her shoulder. With one last look back at Ty and Mac—who each gave her a thumbs-up—she strode toward the officer.

Tall and gangly Officer Quinton had been the one to give her access to some crime-scene evidence a few weeks ago. Getting him to do so hadn't been that hard. Whether she liked it or not, Cassidy was going to find out if that was a fluke or a pattern.

She slid across from him and offered a bright smile. This was so not like her. She'd never been the type to flirt or to care about being popular or getting attention. No, she'd been dedicated to her studies. She'd been immersed in piano practice and Spanish lessons and advanced academic classes.

All things she'd done to make her parents proud. And none of them had ever been enough. Trying to please them was a lesson in futility.

Had they even noticed Cassidy's absence? Did they

care?

The fact that she had to ask herself those questions was a sad testament within itself.

Officer Quinton's eyes brightened when he saw her. "Well, hey you. It's been a while."

"I was hoping we might run into each other again," she started, wanting to puke a little in her mouth.

He grinned, totally buying her story. He leaned back, a new look of confidence sweeping over him—despite the ketchup on his chin. "What's been going on?"

"I was so impressed with the way you and the chief solved that murder on the island earlier this month. Good work." She lowered her voice until she sounded demure and nearly purred.

He beamed with pride. "Thank you."

They hadn't solved that mystery at all. Cassidy had handed the chief all of the answers. She didn't bring that up, however. She didn't need the recognition.

"I heard there might have been another murder," she ventured, tilting her head.

She could feel Ty and Mac watching them, and she cringed. She didn't love having an audience, but shooing them would draw too much attention. She only hoped they weren't enjoying this too much.

Quinton's chest puffed out, and he took another bite of his burger. He didn't seem to notice—or care—that she had nothing to eat or drink. "Maybe. We don't know yet. But there's definitely some weird stuff going on."

Cassidy leaned closer, trying to look both impressed and smitten—like one of those women who followed cops around. Badge Bunnies were what people called them. "Like what? Are you allowed to tell me?"

He glanced around before turning back to her with a glimmer of excitement in his eyes. "Not really. It's all hush-hush."

"All of it is? Or just part of it?"

He seemed to consider her question. "Well, I guess not *all* of it."

"Can you share anything? Because I'm thinking about leaving this place, especially if there's been another murder. I came here to Lantern Beach because I thought it was safe."

"As long as you don't hang around the wrong people, you should be okay."

"But what about that man who died? I just bought some cucumbers from his stand two days ago. And now he might be dead!"

"We don't think he's dead," he whispered, stealing another glance around them.

A sparkle of excitement ignited in Cassidy. "You don't?"

He leaned closer. "No, that wasn't his blood we found inside his place. It was someone else's."

Engage ditzy blonde persona . . . and, go! "No way! How do you even know that?"

He shrugged, a gleam of pride in his eyes. "We have our ways."

He probably didn't know—he was just reciting information the chief had told him, based on results the lab had sent in.

"So you mean to say that the produce guy isn't a victim, but he might be a . . . killer?"

He shrugged and picked up a homemade chip. "You didn't hear it from me."

"Oh, no. I didn't hear it from you." Cassidy grinned at him. "You know just how to make a girl feel special, though. And I *love* feeling special."

She might have actually thrown up in her mouth that time.

———

In order not to break her cover, Cassidy sat with Officer Quinton for the rest of lunch. It would look too suspicious for her to return to the table with her friends, and Quinton didn't appear to have seen them come in together. If he did, he gave no indication.

Instead, she watched him scarf down a burger topped with Cajun shrimp and andouille sausage, devour the homemade chips, and even finish off a slice of chocolate and cayenne-pepper cake. She thought Quinton would never stop eating.

Finally, he got a call and stood. "I have a parking violation to attend to. But it's been nice chatting with you, Miss . . . Miss . . ."

She resisted a scowl. He really didn't know her name? "Livingston. But you can call me Cassidy."

He grinned, that glob of ketchup still on his chin. "Maybe we can do it again sometime."

"I'd like that." How far would Cassidy go to make her new persona believable? Would she pretend to date someone in order to not blow her cover? The lines felt so murky. And she was a pretty square person. This lack of definites in her life was making her insane.

As soon as Quinton was out the door, she dropped her smile and made her way back over to her friends.

They grinned as if they'd enjoyed watching the whole thing.

Since Skye had joined them and sat beside Ty, Cassidy slid in next to Mac and picked at her food—jalapeno popper soup with cod, which was now cold.

"Well?" everyone asked.

She shared what she'd learned, watching Skye's expression carefully.

"If it wasn't Buddy's blood then . . ." Skye started.

Cassidy shook her head. "We don't know. I don't think the police know."

"I wish I'd never argued with the man." Skye hung her head. She was the creative type, the kind who was prone to highs and lows. The kind who felt things deeply. This was definitely a low, and she was definitely feeling it deeply.

"The police certainly can't think you're a suspect anymore," Ty said. "When you take into account the time the neighbor reported you to when the police arrived, you didn't have time to do the crime. Besides, if Buddy wasn't the victim, then you have no motive."

"Besides, what were you doing before that?" Cassidy asked. "Do you have an alibi for the morning hours?"

Skye's face darkened ever so slightly. What was that about?

"Of course I do," she said. "I had a meeting."

Something about the way she said it made Cassidy pause. "What kind of meeting?"

"It was a business thing. No big deal."

Cassidy's gaze met Ty's. If it wasn't a big deal, why was Skye being so elusive?

She didn't know. And, to be honest, Cassidy wasn't

sure she wanted to find out.

———

Skye told them she wanted to go back to her produce stand and check her inventory. And Ty's father wanted to help him build some new shelves for the storage area beneath his house. All of that was fine with Cassidy because she really wanted a little time alone to process everything she'd learned.

After Ty drove her home, Cassidy walked back into her house, locked the door, and plopped on the couch.

So . . . someone else had obviously been in Buddy's house. There had been some type of altercation, if Cassidy had to guess. But Buddy wasn't the one injured—the other man had been hurt.

Both of them had disappeared. Skye had shown up, pushed through the door, and fallen into the pool of blood there. The neighbor across the street had reported it.

So far, Cassidy didn't know who the victim was, what exactly had happened to thus-said victim, what a motive might have been, or any other details.

Talk about a strange investigation.

She comforted herself with the knowledge that Chief Bozeman probably wasn't any further along than she was when it came to finding answers, and he had every advantage at his disposal.

The fact about her phone being taken did bother her, but Cassidy didn't think anyone should be able to trace her. That was the good news. Thankfully, she wasn't a selfie-taking queen or social media butterfly.

The whole produce-stand thing was strange, however.

Why would Buddy put grocery store labels on produce when most people wanted things that were homegrown?

Maybe she'd pay the place another visit.

At that moment Cassidy's phone rang. Her secret phone. She pulled it from the bottom of her purse and saw that it was Samuel. Did he have an update?

She quickly answered, anxious—and partially terrified—to hear why he was calling. "Samuel."

"Cassidy, I looked into that murder that you asked me about—the unsolved one."

"What did you find out?" She sat up straighter, waiting in anticipation.

"The police suspect DH-7 was involved, as you might have assumed. The woman was stabbed in the abdomen several times. There were no witnesses, and the police have no leads. However, they could tell a few things based on the angle from which she was stabbed."

"Like what?"

"Like the fact that her assailant wasn't tall or especially strong. She was possibly a woman."

No, no, no, no.

"Is there a suspected motive?" Cassidy's voice trembled, and she pulled a pillow in front of her.

"Probably a gang initiation."

No, no, no, no.

"When do they suspect she died?" She held her breath as she waited for his answer. She wanted to know, yet she didn't want to know.

"May 2," he said.

The room began to spin. That was the same day Cassidy had woken up covered in blood.

What had she done?

CHAPTER
THIRTEEN

CASSIDY LOWERED her head until it was between her knees, fearful that she might pass out.

What if she had killed that woman?

Cassidy didn't know how flakka made her act. She'd never done any type of drugs before. But if it had the same effect on her that it had on others . . . she could have completely lost her sensibilities and control and . . .

She didn't want to think about it.

Guilt pounded at her temples.

Spontaneously, she jerked her head up. She needed to call Ryan. Though she'd agreed to be in contact only in case of an emergency, this was an emergency.

Was she going to tell him her theory? Maybe. He was a prosecuting attorney. He'd know how to handle this.

And she didn't know who else she could talk to.

Before she lost her courage, she dialed his number and held her breath as she waited for him to answer.

The phone rang. And rang. And rang.

No answer.

Finally his voicemail picked up.

What? Ryan always answered his phone, unless he was in court or in a meeting. But still . . .

Cassidy hadn't talked to him in three weeks.

But if something had happened to Ryan, Samuel would have told her.

She tried one more time, with no answer.

Quickly, she went to the computer and Googled his name. She held her breath, hoping as the results populated the screen, that there was no bad news.

As she scanned each of the news items, she released the air from her lungs. Ryan appeared to be okay. She clicked on several of the articles and paused, noticing a recurring theme in each.

Ryan had hired a new paralegal. A pretty, young thing with long blonde hair and a proclivity to wearing low-cut blouses.

Cassidy shook her head and looked away.

A pretty young paralegal didn't mean anything.

Cassidy had never been the insecure type who got jealous or who stalked boyfriends, fearing unfaithfulness. Despite Cassidy's reassurances to herself, she couldn't help but wonder if there was something going on she should know about.

———

Ty knocked on Cassidy's door two hours later. Rain droplets coated the top of his hair and parka as he stepped inside. She shouldn't feel this happy to see him, but she did. Ty's presence calmed her in ways it shouldn't—in ways that defied logic.

"Believe it or not, it's letting up a little out there," he said.

She shoved those thoughts aside and pulled her sweat-shirt closer. The rain had brought with it unseasonably cool air. "That's good news, especially since I have three inches of water beneath my house."

"At high tide, that's supposed to get worse, unfortunately."

"Great." Elsa might become an ice cream boat if she wasn't careful.

Ty paused and seemed to remember his reason for coming. "My parents want to know if you want to eat with us. I'm cooking. I would have called but . . ."

"My phone is missing." She frowned.

"Yep. That. You going to buy a new one?"

"Eventually. Maybe." Cassidy paused, her heavy and unsettled thoughts bleeding into this situation as well. "Are you sure you don't want to tell your parents the truth, Ty?"

His face tightened. "Do I? Yes, I do. And I've started to several times. Usually right about then my mom launches into a story about how happy she is I finally met a nice girl."

Cassidy nibbled her bottom lip. "I see."

He touched her arm. "Look, I totally understand if you're done with this. I shouldn't have pulled you in the middle of it. And, even if we are officially dating for just this week, there's a part of my conscience that doesn't feel right about this. I don't make a habit of lying to people I care about."

At least there was that.

"Listen, let's give it a few more days." Cassidy's

compassion won out over common sense. "But if the opportunity comes up to talk to them, maybe you should let them know that we're not as serious as they might think. I mean, to some people hiding in a produce stand together might be a date. But to most people . . ."

Ty chuckled. "I don't know. Run-of-the-mill dating isn't that interesting. But cuddling under the counter . . ."

"We weren't cuddling."

He smiled. "We practically were."

"No, you were just sitting incredibly close. You apparently have boundary issues."

"It was a small space. What was I supposed to do?"

Cassidy smiled. "Well, our next date I want flowers and candlelight."

He stepped closer, close enough to prove her boundary issue theory. "I like the way you think. Since we're dating this week, I should take you up on that."

She felt her cheeks heat as she stared up into Ty's luminous brown eyes.

Cassidy was in trouble. Because she halfway liked the idea of going on an actual date, even though she knew the end result would only be disastrous.

———

Dinner had been lovely, as had dessert—some kind of trifle with chocolate cake, pudding, whipped cream, and toffee. Ty really was an excellent cook, and the freshly caught tuna was top restaurant quality.

After dessert, they'd moved to the deck for coffee. The rain had cleared for a little while, and pockets of smeared pastels from the sunset-filled the sky. Cassidy and Ty leaned against the railing, Kujo beside them, as Ty's family reminisced.

"It's a good thing Frank had his camera ready," Del said. "Because that seagull swooped down and snatched the fish right from our line. And it was at least thirty inches! Biggest red drum I've ever seen."

Ty shrugged. "No other fishing experience has quite lived up to that one."

Cassidy chuckled. "I can imagine."

Abruptly, Del stood and held up her phone. "Speaking of pictures, I need to get a picture of you two together for my mantel."

Cassidy forced a smile before giving a look to Ty. He looked just as reluctant as she felt. Despite that, they squeezed together. Just one picture couldn't hurt.

"Oh, that's just beautiful," Del said, snapping a photo with her phone. "With the sun setting behind you like that, it could be a magazine cover. But now I need a real picture."

"What do you mean?" Ty tensed beside her.

"Act like you like each other." Del motioned for them to scoot closer together.

"Of course we like each other." Cassidy offered a falsely cheerful smile again.

"No, *act* like you really like each other. Give her a kiss."

Panic swirled through Cassidy. A kiss? No way, no thanks, no how. That was *not* part of this deal.

"She's a little shy," Ty said, poking her in the ribs.

"I'm not shy," Cassidy insisted.

Why had she said that? It was the perfect excuse for not showing any PDA.

"Then let's see a kiss." Del wagged her eyebrows. "Make this old woman happy."

Okay, smarty pants. What's your excuse now? Should have stuck with being shy.

"Just one picture . . ." Del waited patiently.

Cassidy looked up at Ty, waiting for him to make an excuse. His gaze met hers, a surprising—and jolting—look there. Before she realized what was happening, Ty's hand slipped around her waist and he pulled her closer.

"One little kiss couldn't hurt . . ." he murmured.

What had he just said? Before Cassidy could let the thought settle, Ty's lips met hers. Gently yet firmly. Soft yet somehow loaded.

The jolt of electricity that swept through Cassidy curled her toes.

Her toes curled? Did that really happen in real life? She thought it was just on TV and in books.

Because when she'd kissed Ryan, she'd never felt such a flash of intensity or longing.

As soon as the kiss started, it was over.

Cassidy tried not to stumble as Ty stepped back. Definitely tried not to make eye contact with Ty. Because her whole world felt as if it had been rocked . . . and she didn't know what to think about that. Kisses . . . well, kisses shouldn't make her feel that way.

"Oh, that's just perfect!" Del stared at her camera, a wide grin across her face. "The storm cleared for just long enough to smear some pretty pinks and yellows and blues in the background. You're going to want to frame this one."

Cassidy hardly heard her. Her mind felt close to short-circuiting.

She'd just kissed Ty. No, he'd kissed her. Maybe they'd kissed each other. She didn't know. But she did know that she was dating Ryan.

But she was also undercover and trying not to blow her new identity.

The conflicting thoughts nearly made her head spin. Life shouldn't be this complicated. Most people's weren't.

Perhaps Cassidy wouldn't feel so guilty if she hadn't enjoyed it so much. It seemed so beyond the realm of possibility, especially since she and Ty could hardly stand each other . . . right?

"I'll send you both a copy," Del said, punching something in on her phone.

She'd gotten Cassidy's phone number earlier.

But . . .

"I actually lost my phone," Cassidy said.

If whoever had taken Cassidy's phone saw that picture pop up on her home screen, he'd know who'd been in the produce stand. All of her texts showed up as push notifications first, no password needed.

"Oh, well." Del shrugged and slid her phone into her pocket. "I just sent it! Hopefully you'll find your phone soon because I'd hate for you to miss out on that picture."

Cassidy's stomach clenched again. Finally, she stole a look at Ty. His pensive expression reflected her own feelings.

This wasn't good—on so many levels.

CHAPTER
FOURTEEN

CASSIDY TRIED to catch her breath as she pointed behind her. She needed a moment to gather her thoughts. And she couldn't do that around Ty right now.

"You know, I should probably run home and check on my friend who's staying with me," she said, her cheeks still flushed. "I hate to be rude, but . . ."

Del waved a hand in the air. "You're not being rude at all, Cassidy. Go on and go. I don't believe in shackling the people I love. I want them to have freedom."

Had Del just said that she loved Cassidy? Certainly she'd misspoken. She hardly even knew Cassidy.

Cassidy's parents had only told her they'd loved her twice in her memory. Once was when she'd been in the hospital with pneumonia at nine years old. The doctors were afraid she wouldn't make it. Her nanny had brought her in, and Cassidy wasn't sure how much time had passed, but it felt like hours before her parents finally arrived.

Gertrude, her nanny, hadn't been able to reach them

because her dad was in an important, no interruptions style of meeting, and her mom was having some type of procedure done—probably Botox—and hadn't had her phone on her.

The second time they'd said it had been when Lucy died. At the funeral, her mom had leaned toward Cassidy and whispered that she loved her.

It had been so subtle that Cassidy had wondered if she'd imagined the words. Or if she longed to hear them so badly that she'd engaged in wishful thinking.

Cassidy hadn't watched TV much as a child, but from the little she'd seen, the commercials had stood out to her the most. Each one had images of a perfect family with a loving mom and dad who took their kids to the park. Whose faces beamed with pride as their kids graduated from high school. Of parents who offered grace and forgiveness when their child scribbled on the walls or got involved in a fender bender.

Cassidy's parents had been none of those things. They'd mostly been absent, but the times they were with her, they weren't really with her. Her dad was on the phone with work. Her mom was planning parties or redecorating her house, as she seemed to do every two years.

It was amazing that Cassidy had the capacity at all for warmth and connection.

At least Gertrude had shown her love and affection. Cassidy still thought of her nanny as a second mom, though in truth she was more of a mom than Cassidy's real mother had ever been.

If she married Ryan one day, she was going to be following in her parents' footsteps. Wasn't that what people did? They gravitated toward what they knew because, even if the familiar was bad, it was also comfortable and expected. Though Cassidy had vowed not to be like that, she was headed exactly down that same path.

That realization wouldn't leave her. It had captured her thoughts earlier this week as well, almost like some kind of wisdom from someone bigger than herself was speaking to her conscience.

"Let me walk you back." Ty started toward the steps with Cassidy, a hand on her back.

Oh no. More time with him? That was a terrible idea.

Cassidy paused and pressed her hand gently against his chest. "You know what? Stay with your parents. I'll be fine."

Ty opened his mouth like he wanted to say more. But then shut it again and nodded as his gaze searched hers. "Are you sure?"

"Yeah, we can talk later, okay?"

He nodded again, though it looked reluctant. Relief rushed through Cassidy. Right now, she just needed space from him—at least until her head stopped spinning. Ideally, she'd forget that kiss all together. Not likely, though.

She rushed through ankle-deep water—a mix of rain and ocean overwash—to her house. Once inside, she found a note from Skye. "I'm tired, so I turned in early. See you in the morning."

Cassidy had never taken Skye for someone to turn in so early, but stress could probably cause that also. Cassidy wasn't going to complain about it right now, because she needed some time alone.

She sat on her couch and pulled her purse into her lap.

Her hands trembled as she pulled out her hidden phone. She needed to talk to someone.

Ryan.

This wasn't about Ty. Not really. Sure, Cassidy had never felt such a jolt from a simple kiss before. And the fact that she was feeling anything toward Ty should be a sign that she wasn't ready to be with Ryan.

This phone call was about the fact that Ryan had chosen to hide his relationship with Cassidy, putting his upcoming election for prosecuting attorney first. It was about the fact that Ryan was a workaholic. That they were dating more because of logic than any type of connection.

There needed to be a balance, didn't there?

With her heart lodged firmly in her throat, Cassidy dialed Ryan's number. Again.

She remembered the pictures of Ryan with his new paralegal. Did that woman have anything to do with his inability to call Cassidy back?

Cassidy wanted to say no, yet something inside her screamed yes. She had no evidence. No proof. Just pure gut instinct.

The phone rang and rang and rang some more. But there was no answer from Ryan.

As the line went to voicemail, she cleared her throat. This was never the way she'd intended on doing this, but Ryan had left her no other choice.

"Hey, it's me. Listen, I haven't been able to get in touch. I hope everything is okay. I just wanted you to know . . . you and me . . . we just need to call it quits. I think we've both known it for a while. There are a lot of reasons, starting with the fact that we've been apart more than we've been together. My time away . . . well, it's shown me some sides of myself that I need to change. I think it would be better if we went our separate ways. Sorry to leave this as a message, but I haven't been able to catch up with you. I wish you the best, Ryan. Bye."

When Cassidy hung up, a huge weight felt like it had been lifted from her chest.

It was time she made some changes in her life. Cassidy didn't want to go back to Seattle and act like the same person she'd left as. That wasn't even possible.

Her time in DH-7, her time here on Lantern Beach . . . both had changed her.

And she needed to figure out what that meant.

———

Ty felt as if he'd touched electricity. He'd tried to wipe his feelings from his expression as he'd stood there with Cassidy on the deck, but the woman was insightful. Surely she'd seen the surprise—and maybe even enjoyment—on his face after their brief kiss.

Had she felt the same thing he had?

All those thoughts had come to a halt when he realized his mom had texted the picture to Cassidy's phone. Whoever had taken the device had just been handed irrefutable evidence about who they were.

Which meant he needed to keep an eye on Cassidy.

If the man who'd come into the produce stand had been the one behind the blood at Buddy's place . . . then Cassidy—and Ty—could both be targets now.

"Cassidy's nice, Ty," his mom said as they washed dishes. "Very nice."

Guilt panged through him again. *Tell her the truth.*

Yet it had been so long since he'd seen his mom this happy. He hated to ruin that. His mom just wanted Ty to have what she and his father had together. They were happy. Best friends. Companions.

But Ty doubted that would ever happen for him. What his mom and dad had was something only a select few experienced. What made Ty think he was lucky enough to be one of those people?

"Cassidy is nice, isn't she?" Ty slipped a platter back into his cabinet.

"Can you see yourself spending forever with her?"

Ty nearly dropped the plate he'd just picked up from the drying rack. "I think you're rushing ahead a little bit."

"Am I? When you know, you know."

A cloud formed over him as his thoughts shifted. "I thought I knew with Renee."

"You know I never liked her from the start," Mom said.

"You've never liked any of my girlfriends." It was true —none of them were ever good enough or right for him, according to Mom. She'd tried to be kind each time when breaking the news to Ty, but her message was always loud and clear: she didn't approve. Now, the one time Mom did approve was with a girl Ty wasn't really dating. Go figure.

"I like Cassidy."

Well, there was that.

"I'm not in a hurry, Mom. We haven't been dating that long." Only two days officially, and that was still question-able. He lowered his voice as his thoughts shifted. "How are you feeling lately? Do you have any more appoint-ments coming up?"

He almost didn't want to ask. He'd rather avoid the

subject. Yet he had to know. He needed to face reality, however ugly it was.

"I have my six-month follow-up next week, as a matter of fact. I already had the blood work done for it before I left. If this one goes well, I'll be considered cancer free."

"That's great." He prayed for good news. He more than prayed for it—he yearned for it with all his being.

"You know how your dad gets all worked up every time these appointments roll closer," she said, lowering her voice. "That was another reason I suggested we come here. I thought it would be a good distraction."

"I'm glad you came, Mom." He kissed her forehead, praying again that the appointment went well. His mom and dad deserved some peace in their lives—a period of walking through the Land of Promise instead of through the desert.

Tell her.

Ty opened his mouth, guilt—rightful guilt—getting the best of him. He'd prided himself in being honest and virtuous. What had he been thinking with this ruse? It was so unlike him.

"But you know what?" His mom turned to face him.

"What's that?" Ty turned toward her.

"I know I'll sleep so much better at night knowing you're not here all by yourself. Man isn't meant to be alone. That's why God created woman."

Ty shut his mouth and shut away his thoughts of confessing.

But that didn't stop the regret from pounding at his temples.

CHAPTER
FIFTEEN

TODAY'S GOALS: PINCH PENNIES
UNTIL THE RAIN CLEARS AND ICE
CREAM SALES RESUME. KEEP
ASKING QUESTIONS. DON'T KISS
TY AGAIN.

CASSIDY WOKE up the next morning feeling more
well-rested than she had in months. She hadn't realized
how much dating Ryan had left her feeling unsettled. But
apparently she'd known deep inside that it wasn't right.
She'd just chosen to ignore those feelings.

She climbed out of bed, hopped in the shower, and
then went to grab breakfast.

The bad weather had let up for a little while, but fore-
casts had said it would be raining off and on all week. This
wasn't boding well for her paycheck. And, yes, Cassidy
needed her paycheck to survive here.

She hadn't had time to secure any money before leaving, and the little she'd had on her would run out quickly
without some supplementation. If worse came to worst,
she could ask Samuel to wire her some funds, but that
wasn't without risks. She'd rather do this on her own.

She grabbed a granola bar and poured herself a glass of
almond milk before sitting at the breakfast bar. As she
glanced out the kitchen window at Ty's house, she spotted

him and his father walking toward the beach with fishing poles in hand.

She smiled at the sight.

That was what family should be.

She looked away and took another bite of her granola bar. She wanted to formulate a plan for today. Unofficial goals: she wanted to track down Buddy Macklemore—or the man who'd looked like him, at least. She might want to pay another visit to that produce stand. And she wanted to know if Buddy had any friends he'd hung out with while he was in town.

If there wasn't some resolution to this soon, she feared Skye might have a breakdown. Her friend wasn't handling the accusations well, and the rain had made it nearly impossible to work at the produce stand and keep her thoughts distracted.

Stay low-key, she reminded herself. Don't draw any unnecessary attention to yourself.

She had to repeat that to herself at least ten times a day.

After she finished her breakfast, Cassidy decided to check on Skye just to make sure she was okay.

She gently knocked at her door. When there was no answer, Cassidy twisted the knob and prodded the door open.

Sunlight filled the room, revealing . . . an empty bed.

An empty bed? What?

Cassidy rushed into the room, looking for a sign of where her friend had gone. As she reached the nightstand, she saw a piece of paper there and snatched it up.

I've gone to follow a hunch. Be back soon. ~ Skye

Cassidy's stomach dropped. Just where exactly had Skye gone?

She didn't like the sound of this.

———

Ty and Cassidy sat across from each other on her deck, not even the balmy wind rushing over them offering any comfort.

They'd called everyone they knew, and no one had seen Skye. Cassidy had even called Skye's niece Serena in Michigan. She hadn't heard from Skye but promised to call if she did.

"Where could she have gone?" Cassidy mumbled.

"I can't believe she would do this." Ty shook his head. "It's just not like her."

At the sound of heavy footsteps, their heads turned toward the noise. Austin appeared, taking the stairs by twos and revealing his work jeans and boots. He was a handyman in the area, and one of Ty's good friends. The man looked like he could host one of those shows on HGTV, with his long dark hair that he pulled back in a ponytail, a fit build, and chiseled cheekbones.

"Anything?" Austin looked wired and ready to pounce at the first sign of bad news. It showed in everything from his voice to his posture.

He cared for Skye, didn't he? Cassidy had known the two of them were good friends. Skye had told Cassidy that she liked the creative, artistic type. Cassidy had never thought of Austin that way, but . . . maybe Skye did. Or was Skye even aware that Austin had feelings for her?

Ty shook his head. "No, no leads so far."

Austin sat down hard in a chair across from them. "So you're thinking she took off last night?"

"She left me a note last night telling me she was going to bed early," Cassidy said. "I thought it was weird that she was constantly sleeping so much, but I figured it was the stress of it all."

"But she really left that note to throw you off, so you wouldn't know what she was actually doing," Ty said. "She has more guile than I thought."

"But her car is still here," Austin said.

"My bike is missing," Cassidy admitted. "The only thing I can figure is that she took it."

"Why would she take your bike instead of her car?" Austin asked.

"That's a great question." Cassidy couldn't figure it out either.

Austin leaned toward them, his concern still wrenching the joy from his eyes. "When was the last time you saw her?"

"Before dinner last night," Cassidy said. She'd stopped by briefly to get a sweater before heading back to Ty's. "Skye seemed a little stunned still but like she was doing okay."

"Maybe we should split up and go around town, asking business owners and anyone else if they've seen her," Ty said.

"Sounds good. I'm in. I'll call Wes. I'm sure he'll help also."

Cassidy grabbed her keys, ready to do her part when Ty stopped in front of her and shook his head. "I'll drive."

Not this conversation. Not again. Why did they seem to have it every time they were together?

"We're splitting up," she repeated.

"We're not splitting up." He pointed his fingers back

and forth from Cassidy to himself, a rock-like demeanor hardening his body.

"But it makes more sense."

He shook his head again. "Not when we consider the fact that your photo went out last night and the person who stole your phone may have seen it."

"Your photo went out also."

"But I can handle myself."

Cassidy wanted to argue that she could handle herself as well, but she knew how that would sound. There was no earthly reason, in Ty's mind, for him to believe she could protect herself in a dangerous situation.

So she had no choice but to comply, whether she wanted to or not. All for the sake of her cover.

"Fine, but I still think I'd be okay."

He leaned closer, not backing down an inch. "Besides, there's still a flood watch and parts of the highway are covered. My truck makes more sense than your sedan."

Again, Cassidy couldn't even argue with him. "Let's go then."

It looked like another bad day for selling ice cream. Poor Elsa was going to start feeling neglected if this weather didn't change.

As if on cue, "The More We Get Together" started blaring from the truck's speakers.

Cassidy shook her head. That truck . . . it was like she had a mind of her own.

Maybe it had something to do with the fact her original owner had been found dead inside.

Cassidy laughed at herself. No, of course not. The thought was crazy.

But if Elsa kept playing music on her own, Cassidy might become a believer.

———

Cassidy and Ty hit several businesses before finally stopping at the Crazy Chefette to talk to Lisa. Their friend met them at the door, her worry obvious amidst the orange splatters on her lab coat. Another food experiment, most likely. Perhaps one that had gone wrong, based on the smell of smoke lingering in the air.

"Anything?" Lisa wiped her hands on a towel before flinging it over her shoulder.

Cassidy shook her head, wishing she had better news. "No one has seen Skye."

"Have you heard anything here?" Ty scooted to the side as a man and woman exited the restaurant, complaining that it was hard to breathe inside.

"I've been asking around, but it's the same," Lisa said. "No one seems to know anything. Granted, business here is really slow right now with all the rain and flooded streets. There haven't been a ton of people in here, but I've asked everyone I've seen."

"Keep asking." Ty's hands went to his hips like a soldier surveying a battlefield. "You never know when something will turn up."

"You guys have tried her phone, right?" Lisa asked, worry lines forming at her eyes.

Cassidy nodded. "Several times. We've also been by the van stand. Nothing."

"I just wish I could leave and help." The lines on her

face deepened. "But two people called in sick with a stomach bug and . . ."

"You're doing a fine job here," Cassidy said. "Just keep talking to people."

"I will." But Lisa didn't look convinced. No, she frowned, and her gaze had a far-off, distracted look. "But I'm having trouble concentrating, if you can't tell. I burned a whole pan of cauliflower bread."

"The smoke should clear soon," Cassidy said.

"And if Mac comes in—" Ty started.

"*When* he comes in," Lisa said. "He's here every day. Not even this smoke will drive him away."

"Let him know what's going on, okay?" Cassidy continued.

"I'm sure he'd love to help," Lisa said. "Did you call the police?"

"We talked about it, but we haven't yet," Ty said. "They probably won't do anything. There's no evidence of foul play, and Skye left a note. They'll probably insist on waiting at least twenty-four hours."

"Yeah, I get that. Please stay in touch. Skye is all I can think about." Lisa handed them bags that one of her servers brought out and then grabbed some menus as a family came in. "Here's some lunch for you both—I didn't burn anything in those bags, but I'm slightly afraid I mixed up the horseradish and mayo. If so, I apologize in advance."

"I'm sure it will be great," Cassidy said.

Ty placed a hand on Cassidy's back to lead her away. Another jolt thundered through her at his touch. Why did he have to have that effect on her? The good news was that

Cassidy could choose to ignore it. Which was exactly what she would do.

Just as they stepped out the door, Lisa called to them, and they paused.

"I've been so distracted that I forgot to tell you that someone came in here last night and showed me a picture of the two of you." Lisa's eyes narrowed in curiosity. "You were kissing . . .?"

The picture of her and Ty from last night? Cassidy's heart accelerated. That was just what they needed.

"It's a long story," Ty said, unaffected by Lisa's question. "Tell us more about what happened."

"This man came in here and showed me that picture on a phone," she said. "He asked if I knew either of you and said he'd found the phone and was trying to get it back to the owner."

The color drained from Cassidy's face. He was trying to find them. What would he do when he did? "What did you tell him?"

"I told him if he gave me the phone, I'd return it to you. He didn't seem to trust me, though, because he held onto the device even tighter before putting it back in his pocket."

"And then?" Ty asked.

"I told him you sold ice cream around town, to look for your truck. It seemed safe enough. I didn't give him your name, though. Just in case."

Cassidy's lungs tightened even more. "What did this man look like, Lisa?"

She shrugged. "He was tall and overweight with ginger hair."

Ty stole a glance at Cassidy. "You mean, it was Buddy Macklemore, the man who owned the produce stand?"

Lisa shook her head, worry etched into the lines around her eyes. "No, I know what Buddy looks like. The man looked similar, but it definitely wasn't Buddy. He didn't give me his name."

It wasn't a lot, but at least it was something to go on.

Who was that man? And what was his connection to all this?

That was what they needed to figure out.

CHAPTER
SIXTEEN

CASSIDY AND TY were both quiet—and stunned—as they sat in his truck after talking with Lisa. They munched on their food—shrimp salad wraps with mango jalapeno salsa. Lisa had added some homemade potato chips and seltzer water also.

It was still gray outside, but it wasn't raining at this very moment. The dreary weather was beginning to take a toll on everyone, it seemed. Sunny skies seemed like something they'd never see again.

Keep your eyes to the sun, and you'll never see the shadows.

"That guy's trying to find us," Cassidy muttered, pulling her arms across her chest. She wasn't necessarily anxious, but she needed to act like it.

"The question is: what's he going to do when he finally does?" Ty rubbed his jaw.

"Precisely."

"And who is this guy?" Ty continued, his hand flying in the air.

"We need to find someone who knew Buddy and can

answer a few questions for us." It was the only logical solution.

"How are we going to do that?"

Cassidy tapped her finger against her knee in thought. "I say we talk to the nosy neighbor again. Maybe he saw something."

"It's worth a shot, and I don't have any better ideas."

Ten minutes later, they stood at the front door of the man staying across from Buddy's rental. Sissy answered on the third ring, looking as skittish as ever.

"Can't you just let a guy have a quiet vacation?" he asked, taking a bite of his apple. "And who are you two? The volunteer sheriffs in town?"

"We're two people who are concerned about a friend," Ty said. "And we have a few more questions."

The man had the audacity to sigh. "Fine. You have five minutes. And then I'm getting back to my book. I just got to the part where the hero is about to die at the hands of Nazi terrorists who were sucked into the twenty-third century. Did I mention they're also vampires? It's a fascinating read."

Cassidy didn't even know what to say about that one.

"But please come in before you make me some kind of target," he said. "I don't want anything to do with this."

Ty and Cassidy stepped inside his place but didn't go any farther than the entryway.

Sissy turned to them, his face puckered like he'd sucked a lemon. "Now, what do you need?"

"Did you see anybody else over at the house across the street?" Ty asked, taking the lead. "Besides Buddy—the man who was renting it—and the girl you called the police on?"

"And you two. I called the police about you two also. And your little white-haired friend." He smirked.

That would be Mac.

Cassidy fought the urge to roll her eyes. "Besides us. You said there were less-than-savory characters coming and going."

He let out another sigh and tossed the apple into a nearby trashcan. "I suppose there was one other person I saw over there who seemed identifiable, now that you ask. Not that I'm nosy or anything. Like I said, I just like to read."

"Who'd you see?" Ty put his hands on his hips, looking every bit like a strapping Navy SEAL who'd gone up against terrorists.

Cassidy could sense Ty's patience dwindling with every strange thing this oddball said.

"There was this one man who stopped by a couple of times. He was bald and broad. Kind of reminded me of a bulked-up version of Popeye. He even had a huge anchor tattoo on his forearm."

Ty straightened, as if the description rang a bell. "He's the only one you saw?"

"There were others, but he was the only one who was distinguishable."

"Did this man do anything strange or that caught your attention?" Cassidy asked, trying to get all the information she could.

Sissy shook his head. "No, I can't say he did. But who knows what was going on inside that place. Something deadly, obviously. When I let myself theorize, it has something to do with terrorists and zombies. That's the danger of reading. Fiction and reality sometimes get confused."

"Thank you." Ty took Cassidy's arm and led her back to the truck.

"I had more questions for him," she said, slowing her steps.

"I know who that man is, Cassidy," Ty said. "And I want to go pay him a visit."

————

Ty and Cassidy sat in the parking lot of the marina where Jimmy James worked as a dock hand. He wasn't here, but one of his coworkers told them he'd return soon. He'd gone to pick up some paint for one of the boats.

Ty had explained to Cassidy that he knew Jimmy James from church and that the man was rough around the edges but seemed to have a good heart. They'd decided to wait for him to return.

But after all the preliminary information had been shared, an awkward silence stretched between them. Cassidy stared at the marina, at the tall sails from some of the boats. At the bustle of people coming and going from them. At the well-used dock that was full of ropes and buckets.

Overall, the place was clean and neat—certainly the people who owned the million-dollar vessels wouldn't expect anything less.

The water behind the marina was gray and turbulent, yet it seemed fishing enthusiasts couldn't wait to get out there and see what they could catch.

Ty shifted as they waited. "Look, about what happened yesterday—" he started.

Cassidy quickly held up a hand, jittery inside at the

thought of talking about their kiss. "I get it. We were just playing a part."

Ty shifted and rubbed his neck. "Right. I didn't mean to put you in that position. I should have tried harder to come up with an excuse."

"I take full responsibility for my actions. I'm a big girl, and I didn't have to agree to do this."

He stared out the window. "I tried to tell my mom the truth, but then she told me she was happier than she'd been in a long time, and that she really liked you, and that she and my dad were nervous about another checkup she has next week."

Cassidy reached over and grabbed Ty's hand. She squeezed it, her heart pounding with compassion as her soft fingers intertwined with his rough, thick ones. "I'm so sorry, Ty. I can't imagine watching a loved one go through all that she's been through."

To her surprise, Ty squeezed her hand tighter. "It's been tough. I've wondered many times if I should move back to Texas to be closer to her."

"And?" Cassidy licked her lips. His logic made sense. But there was something about Ty that seemed to fit here on Lantern Beach like the place wouldn't be the same without him.

Which was silly. Because Cassidy didn't plan to stay here forever. Not even for a long time. Just for a few more months until the trial.

"You heard her last night," Ty said. "She doesn't believe in shackling, as she says, the people she loves. She wants me to be happy, and she knows how passionate I feel about starting this home for wounded veterans. Lantern Beach is a prime area for something like that since so many military personnel are in this general vicinity."

"Maybe she could come stay here then. Has she ever considered that?" It seemed like a good solution.

"That's a great question. I always figured she wouldn't want to stay here. I mean, if she has an emergency medical situation, it's not easy to get to a hospital."

"Well, maybe it's something to keep in mind," Cassidy said. "It's obvious your mom and dad adore you."

"I really couldn't have asked for better parents."

Ty's words caused Cassidy's heart to twist. Did he even realize how lucky he was to be able to say that?

Before Cassidy could respond, Ty tensed. "There he is. Let's go see what Jimmy James has to say."

CHAPTER
SEVENTEEN

"JIMMY JAMES!" Ty called, stepping toward the man as he emerged from a truck with a paint can in hand. "Can we talk?"

The man, who looked just as Sissy had described him, paused. When he saw Ty, he seemed to relax—slightly.

But seeing the man in person added a new dimension to Sissy's description. Jimmy James just looked scary. Really scary, in an evil Popeye type of way.

Ty didn't seem to notice or care as he hurried up to meet him on the dock.

"What's going on?" Jimmy James eyeballed Cassidy before his shifty gaze returned to Ty.

"Listen, our friend has found herself in some trouble," Ty started. "And we're trying to find some answers. We were hoping you could help."

"I don't know what I can do, but okay." He set the paint can down, his burly arms flexing as he waited.

"We think this trouble is connected with a person

named Buddy Macklemore," Ty said. "Do you know him?"

Jimmy James's gaze shifted yet again, a sure sign this guy could be trouble.

Cassidy held back, knowing she'd look too suspicious if she jumped right in on this one. Normal people didn't confront men this big and scary looking.

"Yeah, I know him," Jimmy James finally said. "What about him?"

"Would you mind telling us how you know him?" Ty didn't look uncomfortable at all by the man.

Just one more thing to admire about him. Cassidy guessed when you were a Navy SEAL you went up against even scarier guys. He probably knew twenty ways to kill someone and how to cover it up.

"He came to me with some business," Jimmy James started. "That's how I know him."

"What kind of business?" Ty asked.

"He needed some help getting things to and from the island. And I know your next question—what kind of things? I didn't ask. Figured it wasn't my business." Jimmy James talked like a tough guy with short, rough syllables and words that sounded like grunts.

"Were these things you helped him get to and from the island large? Small? Heavy? Light?" Ty asked, turning away from a sweep of rain that blew across the water.

It was like Ty had read Cassidy's mind because that would have been her question also.

"They were big boxes," Jimmy James said. "If I had to guess, they were filled with his produce. Nothing suspicious about that, right?"

"Since he owns a produce stand, I guess not," Ty said.

"But most people who order stuff here on the island have it delivered by the trucks that come into town every day. You were transporting things by boat?"

"That's right. He had some guys waiting at a marina in Ocracoke. I went over, picked the shipment up, and brought it back."

"Where'd you take it once you got there? To the marina?" Cassidy asked, unable to stay quiet any more.

"Nah, I took the delivery to this little plot of land off the highway here in town."

Little plot of land? The one that they'd gone to based on the address scribbled on the paper Ty had found?

"Was it between the general store and the campground?" Cassidy asked.

"It sure was," Jimmy James said.

Cassidy knew one thing for sure. She needed to go back to the produce stand again. The sooner, the better.

———

Just as before, Ty and Cassidy parked across the street from Buddy's and ran through the rain that had just started falling again.

No one was at Buddy's Produce, which was a good thing.

After Ty picked the lock, they slipped inside the little door leading to the shed. Ty hooked up the lights that he'd unplugged last time they were here.

"This time, let's take turns keeping lookout for any visitors," Ty said. "I'll take first shift."

"Sounds like a plan."

The smell hit Cassidy as she stepped farther inside.

Going on day three of not being opened had obviously produced some rotten fruit and vegetables. She pulled her T-shirt over her nose.

"What do you think is here?" Ty said, turning away from the front door. "We already know these aren't homegrown."

"Would Buddy really have been so secretive about that?" Cassidy asked. "He said having Jimmy James deliver his stock was a better deal financially, but I think there's more to the story."

Ty peered out the door. "Someone just pulled up, Cassidy."

He closed the door and locked it before cutting the lights, leaving them both in total darkness.

As footsteps pounded across the little porch out front, Cassidy froze.

The door handle turned.

Cassidy held her breath and stepped closer to Ty.

She had her gun, but if she used it, she might blow her cover. Still, she'd rather blow her cover and live than die due to a crime that she hadn't solved.

Ty reached behind him, his hand skimming Cassidy's hip as he scooted backward. She could feel his muscles bristle.

They both seemed to freeze as they waited.

Then someone knocked. "Are you open? Anyone here?"

Cassidy released her breath at the scratchy voice. It sounded like a senior citizen had come by to buy some produce. Not a vicious killer.

As relief swept through her, she leaned her forehead against Ty's back. He turned toward her, and, as her eyes adjusted to the light, she saw the grin curling the corner of his lips.

His very supple lips.

Her throat went dry at the thought.

Ty leaned closer. "I think we'll be okay."

He was talking about the produce stand and the woman out front.

Not about the two of them. Together as a fake couple. Of course.

Then why did Cassidy's heart race so much? Why did she want him to kiss her again? Not a staged kiss this time, but a real one?

The two of them lip-locking again was a terrible idea.

Her hands rested on his chest. How had they even gotten there? And when had his hands wrapped around her waist?

When Cassidy caught his gaze, she saw the look. The desire in his eyes.

She took a step back, needing to buy some more time before she did something she'd regret. Her hip hit the counter and a cantaloupe rolled off, splattering on the floor.

She glanced down, scolding herself for being clumsy.

Then she realized that wasn't any ordinary cantaloupe.

No, a bag of drugs had been hidden inside.

CHAPTER
EIGHTEEN

CASSIDY SCOOTED BACK until she found the light switch. She flipped it on, desperate to see if her eyes were deceiving her.

They weren't.

There in the middle of the remains of the cantaloupe was a plastic bag full of loaded syringes.

"I think we know what all of this is about now." Ty squatted down to examine the bag better, using the edge of his button-up shirt to pick it up. "Wonder what this is?"

Cassidy could hardly get the words out of her mouth without choking on them. "Flakka."

Ty's gaze caught hers. "Flakka? Are you sure?"

She nodded, numbness spreading through her extremities. Her head swirled, and she feared she might pass out.

Did that mean DH-7 was here on Lantern Beach? This drug was their bread-and-butter. It was what they were best known for. But she hadn't realized it had reached the East Coast already.

"We're going to have to call the police," Ty said.

He picked up another cantaloupe and removed the sticker. Sure enough, a hole had been cut in the top. That was why Buddy had needed the roll of stickers. He'd used them to cover up the hole he used to insert the drugs into the fruit.

"Of course," Cassidy said. There was no way they could not report this. Even Chief Bozeman couldn't refute this evidence.

Ty's gaze remained on her as he pulled out his phone and dialed. He muttered a few things into the receiver before hanging up. "They're on their way."

She nodded, still feeling stiff and out of sorts. Too many bad memories rushed at her. Enough that she felt like she might throw up or pass out or both.

"Cassidy?" Ty studied her without apology.

As their gazes met, Ty reached for her and wrapped her in his arms.

Cassidy wasn't even sure what he murmured as he tucked her head beneath his chin. She just knew it sounded gentle and reassuring.

She'd made up a story when Ty had asked her about the tattoo behind her ear. She'd told him that members of DH-7 had abducted her, injected her with flakka, and she'd woken up with the lightning tattoo behind her ear. It was partially true. True enough, she supposed. What she wouldn't give to tell him the whole truth, to have someone to talk to about the experience.

She leaned into Ty's strength, relishing the feel of his arms around her.

How had they only known each other less than a month, yet Cassidy felt like it had been much longer? How was it that Ty drove her crazy most of the time, but the other half of the time . . . she couldn't stop thinking about him?

At the sound of a car pulling up outside, Ty stepped back. But he didn't let go. No, he took Cassidy's hand and led her outside.

And for once, she was okay with letting someone else take the lead.

———

As Ty talked to the police, Cassidy let her gaze roam the produce stand. She'd only gotten started earlier when she'd discovered that cantaloupe.

She now realized that boxes were missing. Boxes that had been here yesterday. Somehow, whoever took them must have missed this piece of fruit that now lay splattered on the ground, as well as the one they found the hole in.

But suddenly everything started to make a lot more sense.

How did Skye fit in to this? Where was she? And the bigger question: was she okay?

"Tell me again why you were here," Chief Bozeman said.

"Just checking out what Buddy was selling," Cassidy said. "There's no crime in that."

"The place isn't open."

"Now we know that," Cassidy said. "Besides, if we hadn't come, we wouldn't have discovered the fruit."

The chief leaned closer. "You still think your friend is innocent, don't you?"

"Of course we do," Ty said.

"Did she tell you she has a criminal record?" Satisfaction lit Bozeman's gaze.

"Don't be ridiculous." Cassidy crossed her arms, not taking the bait. No way did someone as sweet as Skye have a record.

"Skye isn't the same person," Ty said, loyalty edging into his voice.

Wait . . . it was the truth? And Ty knew about it?

"She's looking more guilty all the time," Bozeman said.

"Well, she's missing," Cassidy said.

"Missing or did she run away?" The chief's gaze held challenge.

She'd left a note. Cassidy couldn't exactly proclaim foul play. But there was more to this story. She knew it.

"She's not guilty, and we're going to prove it," Cassidy said.

Ty put a hand on her back. "If you're finished with us . . ."

Bozeman eyed them both before nodding. "Just don't go too far."

Ty led Cassidy farther away. Before he could say anything, his phone buzzed. He looked at the screen.

"My parents want to take us to dinner in a few hours," he said. "I'll tell them no. We need to keep looking for Skye."

"Actually, dinner isn't a bad idea. Maybe it will give us a chance to clear our heads. Plus, if we're in town, we can keep our eyes and ears open. Talk to people maybe."

"You might be right." He still seemed hesitant. "Let me just check in with Austin first."

He called his friend, who had no updates either. It was

like Skye had disappeared into thin air. Austin was going to keep looking and asking questions.

Cassidy closed her eyes as images began to hit her.

Images of a woman in California who looked like Cassidy. A woman who'd been killed, most likely by mistake. Or maybe not by mistake. Maybe DH-7 knew exactly what they were doing and had killed the woman to send Cassidy a message.

What if Skye was somehow caught up in this web that Cassidy had inadvertently created?

She shook the thoughts from her mind. Thinking like that wouldn't help her advance this case. Wouldn't help her find Skye.

But the guilt was there, flooding her mind just like the overwash from the ocean filled these streets.

And, if she wasn't careful, that very guilt would sweep her into strong currents and drown her.

———

Cassidy had just enough time at her house to freshen up. She changed into some jeans, a black tank top, and pulled on her favorite jacket that Skye had given her—a brown leather one. Though it was summer time, the day had turned surprisingly cool, and it would only get cooler as the sun went down.

With ten minutes until she needed to meet Ty, Cassidy checked her burner phone. Ryan still hadn't called.

Had he gotten her message? Was he okay?

Out of curiosity, she hopped on her computer and did another quick search for him. Sure enough, an online newspaper from Seattle had taken a photo of him just this morning at a campaign stop. And there, by his side, was his new paralegal.

So Ryan was okay. He just wasn't returning Cassidy's calls or responding to her.

Irritation snaked up her spine. She knew he was busy, but was he really that busy? And if he cared about Cassidy so much, shouldn't he be concerned that she was actually calling?

She released her breath. She had just enough time to look up one more thing. She typed in Commotio Cordis. Dozens of hits filled the page.

She held her breath as she scanned the mentions.

Commotio Cordis was the nickname some urban youth had given Cassidy after she'd killed Raul Sanders. Cassidy had thrown a softball and hit him squarely in the chest, effectively stopping his heartbeat.

To some, that made her an enemy.

But to people who feared the gang, Cassidy was a hero and now a faceless urban legend. Devotees had started pages. Fan fiction had been written. And one kid had even started a comic strip featuring her as a skilled crime fighter.

She looked at the pictures. In them, she had dark hair, just as she'd styled it while undercover—kind of stringy, starkly black with blunt bangs. She wore some type of black leather outfit, and her bust size was at least four times larger in the anime drawings than in real life. Her waist had also been significantly reduced.

She looked tough and hard-core, like everything a superhero should be.

Except Cassidy was no superhero.

No, she was someone who might have killed an innocent woman in her fight for justice.

What would Ty think of her when he learned the truth? The man who saw things in black-and-white, who fought for the freedom of both America and those who'd been oppressed halfway across the world.

Did he know the girl next door might be a killer?

She squeezed her eyes shut.

Get a grip, Cassidy.

Take each day as it comes. Yet another quote from her Day-at-a-Glance and excellent advice. However, it was easy to spout but harder to live.

She glanced at her watch. It was time to go. If only she could leave behind her problems, as she'd left behind her old life. But no, they'd been seared into her, and the scars would remain forever.

———

Cassidy enjoyed listening to Ty and his family reminisce about old family vacations and favorite recipes and the big fish that got away.

But she was only half-listening. The rest of the time, her gaze searched the crowd, looking for some sign of Skye or what had happened to her.

They'd gone to the same restaurant on the boardwalk area—The Docks.

Rain hit the tarp above them, creating a pleasant smattering sound. Occasionally, thunder rumbled in the distance. But life continued on. People ate and chatted and enjoyed their day.

That was the irony of life. While some suffered, others

flourished. While some mourned, others rejoiced. Side by side. Within the same pocket of time. Everyone's life continued forward yet the path was flat for some and steep for others.

Cassidy's gaze zoned in on a familiar family four tables away. She saw the man she'd bumped the last time she ate here. And the teen with the lightning tattoo behind his ear.

Cassidy watched them. The family seemed normal enough. The daughter was staring at her phone, the boy was popping peanuts into his mouth, each throw going higher and higher in the air. The parents held a parasailing brochure between them and were in a deep discussion about something.

Cassidy would guess the boy wasn't a hardcore member of DH-7, but instead someone who'd dabbled with a glamorized version of being a gang member. Cassidy blamed the media and video games for glorifying what it was like. Gangs were nothing to be played with.

After she watched them a few minutes, she realized the truth. This boy wasn't here to track her down. No, he was too unassuming. Too relaxed.

Cassidy still needed to be careful around them—around everyone, for that matter—but this boy didn't pose any immediate danger. His biggest mistake was idolizing the wrong people.

"What about you, Cassidy?" Del asked.

Cassidy snapped her attention back to the conversation she hadn't been paying a bit of attention to.

She licked her lips, ready to fess up, when Ty reached under the table and squeezed her hand. She ignored the jolt that went through her.

"Didn't you say you have no plans of going back to

Texas?" Ty obviously realized Cassidy hadn't been paying attention and tried to prod her back into the conversation.

She released her breath. "That's right. I like Texas, but I'm from a small town. There aren't a lot of great job opportunities."

"So do you see yourself staying here in Lantern Beach for the rest of your life?" Del asked.

Cassidy's cheeks heated. "That's a great question. I, uh . . . I don't know. I told myself I'd come here for the summer, just for a change of pace."

"I'm sure your family misses you," Ty's mom continued.

Cassidy shrugged again. "We really aren't that close. My parents . . . they like to work a lot."

"I'm sorry to hear that," Del said. "Really, when everything is stripped away, all you have is your faith and your family. That's what my life has proven, at least."

Faith and family?

Two things Cassidy didn't really have in her life. Could that change? Could her life do a one-eighty?

She didn't know.

Del reached for her ear and gasped. "My earring! It must have come off. My grandma gave these to me."

She started searching frantically on the ground for the jewelry.

Cassidy stooped low, helping Del and grateful for the subject change.

But what she saw wasn't an earring.

No, just a few tables behind her, she saw shoes. Shoes just like the ones she'd seen that day at the produce stand.

CHAPTER
NINETEEN

CASSIDY'S GAZE met Ty's under the table, and she mouthed, "He's here."

Ty squinted. "Who?"

"The man from the produce stand," she whispered.

Ty followed her gaze and realization stretched across his face. "We need to talk to him."

"I agree." Just as Cassidy said the words, the man's feet shifted. He stood.

The man who'd taken her phone was going to leave, she realized. She couldn't let that happen—not without talking to him first.

Cassidy spotted the glimmer of an earring in a crack in the cement. She snatched it up, grateful to have located it so quickly. "Found it!"

Cassidy popped her head back up and presented Del with her lost jewelry.

"Oh, what a lifesaver. Thank you, Cassidy. These are my favorite pair."

"Could you excuse me a minute?" Cassidy said,

urgency pressing on her. "I just saw someone I've been meaning to talk to. He has an unpaid ice cream tab."

"By all means, track him down. You can't have people going around not paying."

"I'm going with her." Ty stood. "Just in case he gives her a hard time."

His parents didn't bat an eyelash, just nodded, as if Ty's pronouncement was no surprise. They'd probably raised him to be the chivalrous type.

Ty and Cassidy wove their way through the crowds toward the man as he leisurely walked away. The closer they got, the more Cassidy realized that the man did look just like Buddy. Except he didn't.

He was a little shorter. His eyes were a little farther apart. And his forehead was a little higher.

Brothers? That would be Cassidy's best guess.

"Excuse me!" Ty called, before the man emerged from the awning and stepped into the rain.

The man stopped and turned toward them.

Cassidy expected to see malice in his eyes. Instead, he smiled as if they were old friends. "Well, hello there. I recognize you two."

Okay, that wasn't how Cassidy thought this would go.

"You do?" Ty's hands went to his hips again in his Superman pose.

As the man reached for his pocket, Cassidy braced herself, ready to fight. A gun? A knife?

Instead, he emerged with her phone. "I thought I'd never find you to return this. I found it at my brother's produce stand."

She released her breath. Her phone. That had been easy . . . and unexpected.

"Thank you." Cassidy took her phone back.

The man nodded affably. "Yeah, I found it and figured you'd left it when you went to buy something from Buddy's. I thought I'd never figure out who you were. Great picture of you two, by the way."

Cassidy's cheeks heated as she remembered the kiss.

"Thank you." She held up the phone before slipping it into her pocket. "Strange thing is, we've kind of been looking for you too."

She threw in the "kind of" to sound less uptight.

"No way. What did I do this time?" He smiled, as if expecting something funny or interesting.

Sheesh. Investigations could take surprising turns sometimes.

"I guess you could say we've been looking for your brother," Ty said.

The man chuckled. "Well, who isn't? He's quite the character."

What did that even mean? Cassidy and Ty exchanged a glance, Ty's expression showing he was just as confused as Cassidy felt.

"Do you know where he is?" Ty asked.

"He had to go out of town for a few days," the man said before extending his hand. "I'm Larry, by the way."

Cassidy cautiously introduced herself.

"Do you know where he went?" She reframed the question.

Larry shook his head. "Nope, I have no idea."

"Do you know when he left?" Ty asked. "When was the last time you spoke?"

"Monday afternoon," Larry said.

But Monday morning was when Skye had stumbled

into the house and discovered blood. Something wasn't adding up here.

"Do you realize the police are looking for him?" Cassidy watched his expression carefully for any sign of deceit.

"Why would they be looking for him?" A knot formed between his eyes, just as another round of thunder rumbled overhead.

"You really don't know?" Ty shifted.

Larry shrugged, like he didn't have a care in the world. "No idea. I got into town Sunday night to surprise my brother. I'm staying in a trailer over at the campground—my tastes have never been as expensive as his. Anyway, the two of us were supposed to meet on Monday, but he called and said something with work had come up and he had to go out of town. Said he'd be back by the end of the week."

"Is that right?" Cassidy muttered, nibbling on her lip and trying to fit the pieces together.

Larry's gaze volleyed from Ty to Cassidy. "Is something wrong?"

"I hate to be the one to break this to you, but the police found blood inside his house on Monday morning," Cassidy said. "They've been looking for him ever since."

He chuckled . . . again. A strange reaction after receiving that news. "Well, he's fine. Maybe it was from some deer meat or something. He does like to hunt."

The man was the most optimistic person Cassidy had ever met. If he was deceiving them, he had his act down pat. He was totally believable.

"What's your brother's last name?" Ty asked.

"Wilson. Why?"

Ty shifted. "Why did he go by Macklemore?"

"Probably cause he liked to gamble." He shrugged. "Don't really know, and I never asked."

"One more question," Cassidy said. "Why did your brother move here to open a produce stand?"

"He said that he realized selling fruit on the island was actually a lucrative career, and he wished he'd discovered it earlier. I didn't ask any questions. It made sense to me. Now, if you don't mind, I want to get back, so I can watch the new season of *America's Got Talent*."

———

Ty leaned closer to Cassidy as they walked back toward the table where his parents sat. He mentally replayed the conversation with Larry. "That was interesting," he whispered.

"Tell me about it."

The man had been so clueless—and he acted as if he didn't have a care in the world. He'd learned that his brother was missing and possibly a part of a murder investigation, yet he had to rush away to watch his favorite TV show.

Ty had thought when they found the man they'd have more answers. But the only thing they'd really learned was that, according to Larry, Buddy was alive and out of town and pursuing a lucrative business on the island.

Did Larry know about the drugs? He didn't appear to.

They already knew that blood didn't belong to Buddy.

Something else about the conversation left him with questions: the intensity in Cassidy's eyes. It was almost like she'd done stuff like this a million times before. Sure, she threw in a few "maybes" and "kind ofs." But overall, she'd grilled the man like a pro.

Was she just a natural at these types of things? Maybe some people just had that propensity.

But still, Ty couldn't help but feel there was much more to Cassidy Livingston than she let on. And he wanted to discover every one of those details.

His mom put her phone away when Ty and Cassidy reached the table. "Did you get your ice cream money?"

Cassidy smiled as she sat down. "I sure did. Thanks for understanding."

"Of course." His mom's smile slipped. "I just got a call from my doctor's office, and something strange showed up in my blood work. They want me to come in early for my follow-up."

Ty's stomach clenched, and that familiar sense of worry started to creep in. "What do you mean?"

"They said it could be nothing, but they want to go ahead and do a scan a few days early," Dad said. "It's no big deal."

Ty tried to read his dad's face. Could this nightmare really be starting again?

He closed his eyes. *Please, Lord, no. Not again. Cut her some slack. Please.*

"Get that expression off your face," Del said. "None of us knows how long we've been placed here on earth, Ty. And I've determined to be happy with the days I have— whether it's many more years or only weeks. This world isn't the end for me, you know."

He nodded, his emotions bigger than his knowledge right now. "I know. But I don't want to see you suffer anymore. Why don't you stay here so I can take care of you—"

His mom clamped her hand on his arm. "We're not going to make decisions like that, Ty. Let's see what the doctor says first. Then we'll take it from there."

Cassidy's gentle touch on his back eased Ty's muscles but only a little.

He finally nodded stiffly. "When are you leaving?"

"In the morning," Dad said. "I guess we should get back to your place and get packed. I'm sorry to cut this short."

"I'm sorry too," Ty said.

Because when it came to people you loved, you had to make every moment count.

CHAPTER
TWENTY

CASSIDY HAD to tamp down the swell of emotions that had risen inside her faster than floodwaters in a storm. They'd come from nowhere. But hearing about Ty's mom had caused an irrepressible urge to cry.

It made no sense. She hardly knew the woman, and Del's diagnosis was still uncertain.

But Ty's family represented all she hoped for in life, the idyllic dreams she had for her own future. Dreams that she'd hardly realized.

And seeing Ty's concern. Hearing the emotion in his voice.

It had nearly broken her.

Cassidy was quiet on the drive back, and, despite her good sense, she interlaced her fingers with Ty's as she sat beside him. It probably wasn't much of a comfort to him. But she didn't want him to be alone right now.

When they finally got back to their houses and climbed from the car, Cassidy threw her arms around Del's neck. "I'll stop by and see you tomorrow before you leave."

Del gripped Cassidy's cheeks. "There's no mourning, child. We're not going to worry about tomorrow because tomorrow is going to worry about itself."

Cassidy nodded. She'd heard that before. It was on her calendar. But hearing it come from Del brought new meaning to the Bible verse.

"You take care of my son, you hear?" Del's gaze latched onto Cassidy's.

Cassidy wanted to tell Del the truth. Yet she didn't. So she nodded, emotions lodged in her throat.

"I'm going to walk Cassidy home," Ty said, his voice deep and heavy. "I'll be back in a few."

"Take your time," Del said.

They didn't say anything as they walked across the wet sand, but Ty reached for her hand again. Cassidy didn't refuse it. They remained silent as they climbed the steps to her covered deck. It wasn't until they were at the top that Cassidy dared to speak.

"I'm so sorry, Ty." She pulled him into a hug.

He didn't refuse it, nor did he say anything, so Cassidy just held him, her arms wrapped around his neck, and his arms around her waist.

She was about to cry, she realized. Cassidy never cried. Her father had always said it was a sign of weakness.

Not only that, but she felt on the cusp of letting her guard down—something that wouldn't be wise. She had to keep the bigger picture in mind here, but her resolve felt teetering at best.

Abruptly, she pulled away from Ty and turned toward the railing. She stared out at the ocean as she tried to get a grip, desperate not to let Ty see the turmoil in her eyes.

Ty appeared beside her, his arm snaking around her as they stared out at the ocean together.

"It puts life into perspective, doesn't it?" Ty asked softly. "Seeing this big ocean makes me realize how small I am. In the grand scheme of things . . ."

"We're just tiny players," Cassidy finished.

"Yet God's thoughts of us are more numerous than the grains of sand."

Ty really believed that, didn't he? Cassidy wanted to have a faith in something bigger than herself also. What would that be like?

She wiped away the moisture beneath her eyes.

Yep. She was crying. Not just over Ty's mom—though that was a big part. But she was crying for Skye. Crying for the woman in San Diego who'd died because of her. Crying because she understood what it was like to be so broken that she couldn't imagine putting herself together again.

But maybe she could. With some help.

"What are you thinking about, Cassidy?" Ty's voice was soft enough to be a caress.

She swallowed hard, trying to find the right words. Her throat burned. "Have you ever thought that you knew exactly what you wanted, only to figure out you didn't have a clue?"

"As a matter of fact, I have."

The burn in her throat grew warmer, but she didn't dare look at Ty. She kept her eyes glued on the ocean. "What did you do?"

"I admitted I have only one chance to live this life, and I needed to make the best of it."

One chance? Make the best of it?

Ty had pegged her when they'd had ice cream together a few weeks ago and he'd said she was the girl who seemed perfect but who tried too hard. Nothing had ever been good enough for her parents, and now Cassidy never felt like . . . well, she'd never felt like enough.

What would it be like to feel whole? Content? Good enough?

Ty drew her closer. Strangely, his nearness wasn't weird but electrifying. Natural. Comfortable.

His body heat warmed her and tried to draw her even closer into its sheltering coziness.

"Sometimes what we think our future should be isn't what happens," he murmured. "Sometimes there's something better in store."

Cassidy's throat felt raw and achy. Better? Could his words be true? Maybe there was more to her future than the fast track to success. Maybe the girl who had it all together actually had it all wrong.

All Ty had to do was mutter, "Cassidy," and she turned toward him. Got a glimpse of his eyes. Eyes that were full of compassion and heat and . . . something else that drew her in like no one else's eyes ever had.

The look unnerved her. Thrilled her. Stirred her curiosity.

In the next instant, Cassidy felt Ty's chest against hers, strong and solid and capable. Her hands went to his neck.

And without so much as a prelude, their lips met—hungry. Curious. Impatient.

Just like earlier, her toes curled beneath her as something just short of magical exploded inside her. Cassidy had been kissed plenty of times. But never had she felt like this.

Her fingers brushed the edge of his hairline. Stroked his cheek and neck. Rested on his chest.

In one move, almost like a dance, Ty turned her around. Took three steps back. The shingles of the house brushed Cassidy's back.

What was she doing? The question slammed into her mind.

Using every ounce of her willpower, Cassidy pushed Ty away and took in a deep gasp of air. Her lips burned. Felt swollen. Felt suddenly like they were missing something.

Missing Ty.

She didn't belong here. She had too many secrets— enough to make a spy's head spin. And she couldn't tell Ty any of them.

She put her hands on Ty's chest and pushed him back even farther. "I can't do this."

His lips curled, and he pulled her closer. "You were just doing it. Really well, if I do say."

Her toes curled again. Because he'd just done it really well also. He was a great kisser—

She had to get her thoughts back into focus. If Ty kissed her again, she'd be a goner.

"I . . ." She what? Cassidy never got flustered. But she was now. Really flustered.

And if she stood here much longer—this close to him— she was going to kiss him again. The temptation was more than she could handle.

So she did the only thing she could.

Cassidy hurried toward her door, her hands trembling as she reached for the knob.

"I'm sorry," she called over her shoulder. "But I shouldn't have done that."

Cassidy took one last glance back. Ty stood there, confusion obvious in his eyes, in his slumped posture.

But she couldn't let that change her mind. Cassidy had to get away from him. Now.

Before she spilled all of her secrets.

CHAPTER
TWENTY-ONE

TY LEANED against the deck after Cassidy escaped inside, running away as if she was either scared or chased by regrets.

What had happened? He knew that she'd felt something also. Cassidy wouldn't have kissed him that way if she hadn't.

But something held her back.

Ty raked a hand through his hair. He couldn't figure it out now. She needed time. And he needed to get back to his mom. The temporary escape from his worries had been nice . . . until it ended like this.

Memories of Renee filled him. Ty had been burned, and he'd vowed not to put himself in a situation like that again. So what exactly was he doing? Just because he felt a connection with Cassidy didn't mean they should date or be together.

Yet he couldn't get the woman out of his mind.

Feeling a new weight on his shoulders, he started back

toward his house. Halfway there, his phone buzzed. It was Austin.

Ty ducked for cover from the spotty rain before answering.

"What's going on?"

"I'm down at the marina," Austin said. "Something happened I think you should know about."

He braced himself, sensing that the news wouldn't be good. "Go ahead."

"The police just took Jimmy James in for questioning," he said. "It turns out they found a bloody knife on his boat."

"Did the blood match what was found at Buddy's house?"

"They don't know yet. I'm sure they'll test it. But there's more to it. The knife they found? It belonged to Skye."

Ty felt the blood drain from his face. "Are you sure?"

"Yeah, man. I'm sure. It was the one she always used at the produce stand to let people sample her fruit and vegetables. It's ornate, distinguishable. And it's hers."

His night just got a lot worse. "So the police think she's a suspect again?"

"Yeah, I overheard them talking. They definitely think she ran because she's guilty. But you and I both know that's not true. We've got to find her."

"I'm doing what I can." Skye? His mom? He hated being pulled in two different directions. But he had no good leads as to where to search for Skye. Maybe with a good night's rest he would.

"Don't give up. Skye needs people on her side."

"I'm not," Ty said. "No man left behind."

It was his mantra as a SEAL, and his mantra now as well.

————

Cassidy lowered herself on her couch and pulled a blanket over her, waiting for her lips to feel normal again. What had she been thinking? She should have never allowed that kiss. But she had, and now she'd need to deal with the fallout. She added it to her already long list of things going wrong in her life.

Needing to clear her head, she pulled out her phone again, an idea playing in her mind, teasing her and tempting her at the same time.

After nibbling on her cheeks for a minute, she made her choice.

She was going to call Samuel. Cassidy had two favors to ask him. Both required putting herself on the line, but it would be worth it.

"You know every time you call it puts you at risk," Samuel answered. People murmured in the background, making Cassidy wonder if she interrupted a dinner party or a meeting.

"I know," Cassidy said.

"Is everything okay?"

"I don't know. But I need to ask you two things. Both are important."

"Alright. I'll hold off on giving you an answer until I know what you're talking about."

She closed her eyes. "First, I need you to trace a number."

"Trace a number?"

"If I give you someone's cell phone number, I need you to find the last known location of the device." It was the only way Cassidy would find Skye. They were out of options.

"I need a warrant."

"I know you can do it off the books."

He didn't say anything. They both knew her words were true. Stuff like that happened plenty.

"How important is this?" he finally asked.

"Very important."

"Does it pertain to DH-7?"

Cassidy remembered the flakka they'd found and contemplated her answer. "I'm not sure."

Samuel sighed. "I'll see what I can do. What else?"

Cassidy's next request nearly choked her. The words didn't want to leave her lips, but she forced them. "Samuel, when I was undercover, I was injected with flakka. I woke up covered in blood."

"What?" His voice climbed with emotion, and the background noise disappeared. "Why didn't you mention this when we debriefed you?"

She pulled her blanket closer. "I don't know. I was scared. I . . . I just don't know."

He paused before asking, "What happened?"

"I don't know. I don't remember anything. But it was the same day that woman was found murdered." Her voice cracked.

"The one you asked me about?"

"Yes."

"I see."

Cassidy fisted the blanket around her. "Samuel, can

you look into it? I need to know if I had anything to do with her death."

"And if you did?" His words hung in the air.

"Then I expect to pay for my mistakes."

"It's doubtful there would be any charges pressed against you. If you did do it, you weren't in your right mind."

"If I killed someone who was innocent, I deserve to pay for it, whether I was in my right mind or not."

She'd killed Raul, and even his death haunted her. Taking someone else's life was a burden, whether they were innocent or guilty.

Samuel lowered his voice. "Last chance to change your mind. I'm willing to forget you told me this. Just say the words, and we won't open this can of worms."

Cassidy was tempted but only for a second. "No, I need to know, Samuel. I can't live with these doubts anymore."

"Very well then. I'll see what I can find out."

CHAPTER
TWENTY-TWO

Today's Goal: Do whatever necessary to find Skye and nothing else.

CASSIDY SET HER ALARM, so she would wake up bright and early the next morning.

Despite how things ended between her and Ty last night, she'd promised Del she'd be there to say goodbye, and she wouldn't go back on her word.

By the time Cassidy got dressed and walked next door, Ty and his parents were already loading suitcases into the station wagon parked beneath his place.

She could feel Ty's eyes on her as she called good morning and raised her coffee mug in a sleepy-eyed salute.

"Well, there you are, Cassidy." Del paused by the passenger side door, looking pretty and comfortable in her light-pink pants and top. "I was hoping I'd see you before I left."

"I promised you would." Cassidy stopped in front of

her, wondering briefly if Ty had told her anything. He didn't seem like the kiss-and-tell type, nor did Del seem to be holding anything against Cassidy at the moment. "I couldn't miss saying goodbye."

As if to confirm Cassidy's earlier thought, Del pulled her into a long, warm hug. "There's just so much to love about you."

Cassidy chuckled at her enthusiasm and beamed at the compliment. Part of her didn't want to let go. For the past few days, she'd felt as if she was a part of a family. It had been the best feeling in the world . . . but she'd known it would end. She should have been more careful not to get too attached.

"I'll be praying for you," Cassidy whispered. Praying for you? When had she ever said that before?

"I appreciate it, sweetheart. I really do." Del turned to Frank and Ty. "Boys, I think there are a couple more bags up there. Would you two be sweeties and get them for me?"

"Of course," Ty said.

As soon as the men disappeared, Del turned toward Cassidy. Her eyes looked so serious and intense that Cassidy braced herself.

"Listen, Cassidy," Del started. "I know what you're hiding."

The blood left Cassidy's face. How in the world did Del know her secret? Fear pulsed through her veins. Had Del recognized Cassidy from the pictures circulating online? Or had she missed something?

"You do?" Cassidy's lungs froze as she considered how she should react. As she ran through scenarios and protocols and fought panic.

Deny, deny, deny.

Then run, run, run.

It was the only thing that made sense.

Del nodded, her lips drawn together with concern. "You don't have to pretend, Cassidy. I know you and Ty aren't as serious as you let on."

Cassidy released a breath of relief. She and Ty. Of course.

Her mind had gone to the worst places.

If it would have been appropriate, Cassidy would have laughed with giddiness. Instead, she remained straight-faced. "Me and Ty? Why would you think that?"

"I'm a woman. I have intuition. I figured Ty probably wanted me to feel better about him being here alone."

Cassidy didn't say anything for fear of saying the wrong thing. Instead, she waited for Del to continue.

"It's okay, Cassidy. I think it's sweet. And I think the two of you are great together. I haven't seen him look at someone the way he looks at you in a long time. Maybe not ever." She patted Cassidy's cheek. "Just don't break his heart, okay?"

That familiar remorse swirled through Cassidy like a whirlpool in the ocean that destroyed everything in its current. "Okay."

But her promise caused another round of regret because Cassidy knew she could never be with Ty, not with the secrets—the lies—she was hiding.

"And let's stay in touch," Del said. "I have your number now."

Cassidy forced a smile, wishing more than anything she didn't have a whole other life in Seattle holding her back. "I'd like that. I really admire your strength, Del."

"It doesn't come from myself. I have a joy that I choose. I know that whatever my circumstance, there's more to this life than what we can see. It really helps to put life in perspective."

Cassidy wished she could find that joy despite her circumstances.

The men lumbered back downstairs with the rest of the bags, and everyone began hugging goodbye. Cassidy's heart lurched as Ty held his mom close. She couldn't even fathom what they were going through right now.

It seemed like a shame that a family who loved each other so much was facing such a crisis while Cassidy's broken family remained untouched by disease or catastrophe.

Cassidy gave more hugs before waving to Frank and Del as they pulled away.

And then she and Ty turned toward each other, the awkwardness between them more uncomfortable than a blistering sunburn.

"I didn't think you were going to come," Ty said, his eyes full of questions.

"I promised I would."

He shifted, and Cassidy knew exactly where this conversation was going—somewhere she didn't want it to.

"Look, Cassidy, about last night—" he started.

"Could we just pretend it didn't happen?" Cassidy rushed, trying to forget the feel of his lips on hers and the way her heart raced.

Ty stared at her. "That's not going to be easy."

She stepped closer, then realized what a bad idea that was, and scooted back again, nearly hitting the post behind her. "But it's possible."

Ty lowered his voice to a more intimate level as those intense eyes hooked her and reeled her in. "Are you saying you didn't feel what I did?"

Cassidy's throat ached, and her lips tingled as she remembered their kiss again. Their connection. Her overwhelming—but unwelcomed—feelings. "No, I'm not saying that, but . . . I just can't go there right now. I have some things I need to work out."

Ty's eyes were swells of emotion and questions, but he finally nodded. "I understand. And I can respect your choice."

"Thank you, Ty."

Her phone buzzed in her pocket. Her burner phone. She hadn't wanted to miss any calls, so she'd brought it with her.

Cassidy swallowed hard, knowing it was either Samuel or Ryan calling. She glanced at the screen. "Look, I've got to take this. It's . . . from someone back home. We'll talk later?"

"Let's do that. Because Skye is still out there somewhere, and every minute that she's gone makes the bad feeling in my gut grow."

Cassidy's also.

Which was why she needed to take this call.

———

Cassidy waited until she was sure she was out of earshot of Ty before answering. Her hands trembled as she huddled beneath her own home and accepted the call.

It was Samuel.

He was calling at six a.m. Seattle time. What if he had

something bad to report? Her life—her future—would look so different if he did.

But Cassidy had to face the truth.

"Good morning." The words sounded dull as they left her lips, but Cassidy couldn't force any fake cheerfulness. No, not with this conversation.

"Hey, Cassidy. I haven't found out anything yet about your second request about the woman in Seattle. I'm working on it, and I have a decent lead."

As Cassidy's stomach sank, her spirits rose. How could her emotions be so conflicting? At least there was hope for some answers . . . eventually.

"But I was able to trace that cell phone number you gave me."

Cassidy gripped the phone tighter, pausing by her stairs. "And?"

"And I'm going to send you the last known location. The phone is dead now. No signal. But maybe you knew that already."

"An address would be great." More than great. It would be her first decent lead.

"Do I need to remind you about the importance of not blowing your cover?"

She stared back at Ty's house, and regret filled her. She desperately wanted to stop living this life. But she couldn't. Not yet. "No, I remember."

"So when I send you this information, you need to promise to be wise. We need you for the trial, Cassidy. Your testimony is going to send these guys away for life."

"I know. Believe me, I know." The weight of her responsibility pressed on her constantly.

"Okay, then. I'll send the address as soon as I hang up."

"Thank you, Samuel."

As soon as Cassidy hit End, she waited, staring at the screen. A minute later, an address popped up there.

It was on Ocracoke. The next island over. By ferry.

She stole one last glance at Ty's place.

More than anything, she wanted to tell him what she'd discovered. But how would she explain how she got this address?

Cassidy couldn't. At least, she couldn't without explaining a lot more, and she'd just promised Samuel she wouldn't do that.

Besides, she was a seasoned cop. She could handle looking into this. It was what she did—put herself on the line to protect others.

With that thought, Cassidy hurried inside, grabbed her gun, and took off.

CHAPTER
TWENTY-THREE

CASSIDY HAD to wait an hour for the ferry to arrive at the docks and then the trip over to Ocracoke took another forty-five minutes.

All in all, it was taking entirely too long to get to where she needed to be. With every minute that passed, anxiety tried to grip her. Finally, Cassidy arrived at the neighboring island and drove down a long stretch of seashore toward the marina.

Cassidy's gun was stashed in her purse, just in case she needed it. Going solo wasn't her favorite way to approach these things—having a partner to back her up was so much nicer. But that wasn't an option right now.

She parked in a public lot near the bustling village, and, after checking Skye's last known location again, she secured her purse in the trunk. Should she take her gun?

Not yet, she decided.

First, she'd take a lay of the land and decide on a plan of action.

She stepped from her car and took the sidewalk toward the harbor.

In a stand at the end of the sidewalk stood Cassidy's bike. The rusty beach cruiser that Skye had borrowed had been chained there.

Skye had definitely been here.

But where was her friend now?

Cassidy walked over to an old building on the edge of the area, a place with peeling white paint and rusty old boat parts. Using the structure to conceal herself, she peered out.

Four boats were directly across from the bike. Huge boats that probably cost millions. This must be a deep water dock if it could hold boats that large.

Where did she even start? She couldn't charge onboard any of these vessels and demand answers from the owners. But her gut told her that Skye was close.

Maybe Cassidy would just sit tight and watch. It seemed like the only option right now that wouldn't get her arrested or killed.

Before she could take a step, someone grabbed her arm. She started to turn, but, before she could, something pricked her neck. And everything went black around her.

———

Ty pounded on Cassidy's door again. It was no use. She was gone. He'd known she probably wasn't home when he saw that her car was missing, but he wanted to confirm.

He bit back his disappointment—and his worry.

Cassidy didn't have to run her schedule past Ty. Not at

all. She was her own woman, and that was another thing he liked about her.

But they'd been unofficial partners this week. And he was concerned. Something dangerous was going on around this island, and he didn't want to see Cassidy in the middle of it. Elsa was still here, so she wasn't working.

He let out a sigh and tried to recalculate his plans for the day. He had to stay busy or he'd think too much about his mom and her upcoming appointment. Worry would creep in. With every minute that passed, his concern for Skye deepened as well.

He drove past the Crazy Chefette, and Cassidy's car wasn't there so he kept going until he reached the old lighthouse. Austin was working on restoring the place, and Ty sometimes helped him. Since they'd run out of options as to where to find Skye, his friend had resumed his work on this project.

Austin didn't look happy as he pounded nails into the wall. In fact, each stroke of the hammer was twice as forceful as it needed to be. His usually upbeat music didn't play in the background, and even his neck muscles looked tight.

He stopped when Ty walked in.

"Something happened," Austin stated, obviously interpreting Ty's body language.

Ty shook his head. "No, not really. No updates."

Austin let out a sigh and started hammering again, a little harder than necessary. "I couldn't sleep so I decided to get to work. I was hoping there would be an update on Skye."

Ty helped hold up the piece of wood Austin hammered. "I know. Me too."

"Skye didn't hurt that man," Austin said. "I heard the rumors that are circulating—rumors that Skye has a criminal record."

"We both know she does, Austin," Ty said quietly, as if anyone else was around to listen. "She talked about it at Bible study."

"Yeah, but not everyone knows the details. They don't realize that she's changed—really changed."

"It was breaking and entering," Ty said.

If people didn't know the backstory, they might think Skye had been a troublemaker. In truth, she'd broken into her boyfriend's house because she thought he was in trouble. He'd been threatening to overdose after Skye gave him an ultimatum: stop doing drugs or she'd walk away.

Her boyfriend's parents had caught her. They hadn't approved of their relationship, so they'd called the police and pressed charges.

"I was with her before she went to Buddy's house on Monday, you know," Austin said.

Ty's gaze swung toward him. "You were? She said she had a meeting."

"Yeah, she did. With me."

Ty shifted and readjusted his hold on the wood. "Do you mind if I ask what it was about?"

Austin shrugged and swung his hammer again. "No, I already told Bozeman. Skye was thinking about trying to do some updates at the van stand. But, even if I just charged her for the materials, it was still out of her budget."

"Did she want that because she was feeling the squeeze from having competition across the street?"

"I think so. She was having trouble paying her bills and

needed to increase her profit—especially before winter came and all the tourists left."

Ty frowned, realizing just how desperate Skye must have been feeling. "I didn't realize things were so tight."

"Yeah, that Buddy guy really messed her up."

So what did that have to do with his disappearance? Anything?

That was what Ty had been working so hard to find out.

―――――

When Cassidy came to, she was lying prone on the floor with a splitting headache.

She pushed herself up on her elbows, something about the setup all too familiar.

She blinked, trying to let her gaze come back into focus. Where was she?

Carpet scratched her fingertips, and a swaying motion made nausea roil in her.

"Cassidy?" someone said.

She pulled her head up, but the pulsing was worse than ever. She blinked again. Was that . . .

"Skye?"

Skye knelt beside Cassidy, her dark hair falling in her face. "I wasn't sure you were going to ever wake up."

Cassidy forced herself upright to a seated position, but the pulsing and nausea only got worse with each movement. She felt like death. Or worse. If that was possible.

"Where . . . ? What . . . ?" She glanced around, but everything was blurry.

Skye grasped her arms, worry staining her gaze. "I

don't know. We're in a boat. A big one. They threw you in here about three hours ago. You've been passed out the whole time."

Everything started to return to Cassidy. Watching the boat. Waiting. Feeling a prick on her neck.

She'd been drugged, she realized.

All the moisture evaporated from her throat.

Skye thrust a bottle into her hand. "Here's some water. Maybe you should take a sip. You don't look good."

Cassidy's hands went to her head as everything spun. Feeling the bottle in her hands, she took a long drink.

"How did you get here, Skye?" She didn't have time to wait for the haze to clear. She needed answers.

Skye frowned and sat across from Cassidy, pulling her knees to her chest. "Someone wanted to meet with me about becoming an investor in my stand."

There was so much wrong with that statement, but Cassidy tried to give her friend the benefit of the doubt. "Why did he—or she—want to do that?"

"He said they wanted to invest in locals. He asked to meet with me, so we could discuss more."

"No warning bells went off?" Cassidy took another sip of water, wishing the pounding in her head would stop.

"No. I mean, maybe." Skye shrugged, her exotic features marred by red blotches and dull eyes. "Cassidy, I didn't have money to buy any new produce from my growers. It was already tight, but with the rain this week and the accusations against me . . . I was feeling hopeless."

"You should have come to us," Cassidy said. "We would have helped."

"I know. But I know you don't have that much cash either. I mean, you sell ice cream."

Cassidy shrugged, unable to argue. Yet she knew the truth. "We could have figured something out."

"Maybe. But the fact was that this guy's offer sounded like exactly what I was looking for. I left last night so I could meet him."

"Without telling anyone?" Wasn't that the number one rule when meeting with strangers? *Always tell someone.* If it wasn't a rule, it should be. Cassidy had seen too many people—women, mostly—disappear for good when meeting for an online ad or internet dating match.

"He asked that the meeting remain quiet. Said he didn't like to advertise his business deals before the fact. It made sense. I guess." Skye sucked in a shaky breath and stared off in the distance. "So I borrowed your bike."

"Why didn't you take your car?"

"I didn't have any gas. I figured it would be a nice little trip. I biked to the ferry, took it over here to Ocracoke, and then biked to the boat. It wasn't really that bad—except for the rain."

Skye's logic was the least of her concerns right now. "What happened when you got here, Skye?"

"I walked on the boat and into the interior, just like the investor instructed." She swallowed hard, her eyes welling with tears again. "The next thing I knew, a bag was pulled over my head and I felt a pinch at my neck. I woke up down here."

A pinch at her neck? That was what Cassidy had felt also. "Who did this to you?"

Skye's eyes met hers. "I have no idea, nor do I have any idea how to get out of here. These guys threatened to kill me, Cassidy. And now they're going to kill you too."

CHAPTER
TWENTY-FOUR

"YOU HAVE no idea who's behind this?" Cassidy asked, her chest deflating. She'd come this far, yet still had no answers. She'd hoped for more. "Do you know anything about who did this?"

Skye shook her head, her eyes still glassy with moisture. "I wish I did. But, it's like I said, they put a hood over my head, so I couldn't see anything. This guy has men to do his bidding. I didn't recognize his voice."

Cassidy shifted her focus to what Skye might actually know. "Did he say why he grabbed you?"

"He said he wants me to help him with his business."

Cassidy nodded, putting at least two pieces of the puzzles together. "He wanted you to sell his drugs—inside your fruit."

Skye blinked. "He mentioned something about that. How did you know?"

"Ty and I have been doing some investigating. A lot has happened since you left."

Skye drew in a shaky breath. "This guy said that would

solve my financial issues. I told him I wasn't interested, that I didn't do stuff like that."

Cassidy shifted, and everything wobbled. Over all, she felt better. She just needed a little more time. "What happened next?"

"Then he told me he was trying to do it the nice way. But if I forced him to play dirty, he would spread it all over town that I had a criminal record. He said no one would want to buy anything from me. He said he would embellish the police reports and add assault and battery. It's not true, Cassidy."

"I believe you. And you can tell me that story later."

Skye nodded stiffly. "He said he was going to give me a day to think about it. I actually thought I was going to die down here. How did you even find me?"

Cassidy swallowed, her throat still unusually dry. How was she going to explain this? "I . . . uh, I got a lead. It's not important how. But I heard this was your last location. Before I could formulate my next plan of action, I was injected with something just like you, and now . . ."

"Please tell me you told Ty where you were going?" Hope lit her eyes.

Cassidy shook her head as regret filled her. "I wish I had. But I was following a hunch. I never thought . . ."

Skye's gaze latched onto hers. "What are we going to do, Cassidy?"

"We'll figure out something," Cassidy said, taking another sip of water. "Just give me a little time."

———

Cassidy rubbed her neck as she turned everything over again and again in her mind. But there was no time to think too much. No, she needed to move. To observe. To formulate.

The boat was quiet, almost like no one else was here. She doubted that was true, though. Best she could tell, they weren't moving and still sitting at the docks.

As she glanced around, she realized they were in some kind of small bedroom. There were no windows, which made her think they were in the hull of one of those giant yachts she'd seen. The place smelled of lemon polish and saltwater. Maybe even a hint of microwave popcorn.

The walls surrounding the space were a dark wood paneling. There was a bed with a light blue spread on it and a metal headboard. A night stand sat beside it with a small lamp. There was one dresser with a jewelry box on top, and a door to a bathroom in the corner.

Cassidy checked it for a mirror, but there wasn't one. So much for breaking it and using the shards as weapons.

Instead, she went to the door, gripped the handle, and tugged. It didn't give, nor had Cassidy expected it to.

She took a deep breath and leaned against the wall. The drug was still wearing off. Flakka. Why had they injected her? Why not just knock her out? After all, they had no idea how she'd react to the drug. What if she'd gone crazy?

She'd always had strange reactions to drugs, ever since she was a child. Any type of cold medicine knocked her out.

The fact remained that she had no idea how flakka made her act.

Cassidy glanced over at Skye. Her friend sat against

the wall with her knees pulled to her chest. She was shaken. More than shaken. She was on the brink of devastation.

Cassidy had to think of a way out before things turned even uglier.

"How did I act when I first got here?" Cassidy asked.

"You were out."

Cassidy swallowed slowly. "Do you remember when I got here?"

"About one. Why?"

Cassidy had been outside at the marina at around noon —maybe a little after. That meant . . . that flakka knocked her out from start to finish.

A strange relief flushed through her. Maybe the drug just made her black out. That would mean . . . that would mean that perhaps Cassidy hadn't done something foolish while undercover with DH-7. Maybe she'd just passed out. It still didn't explain the blood, but it did make her feel a little better.

The first hint of hope crept into her psyche.

But that didn't dampen the reality of the current situation. She and Skye would both be goners if they didn't get out of here. And, as of right now, this room was locked up like a seaward vault.

As soon as the thought entered her mind, the door opened. Cassidy braced herself for whatever was to come.

CHAPTER
TWENTY-FIVE

TWO BIG BURLY guys with lavish tattoos and arms bigger than Thanksgiving turkeys walked in. Both wore all black and had expressionless faces. Cassidy would guess they were underlings—the brawn and not the brains. She needed to keep that in mind.

"The boss told us to check on you," the bald one muttered.

"Who's the boss?" Cassidy stared at the men. She'd never seen them before. Were they friends of Buddy? Or was someone else behind this? She still didn't know. And she *hated* not knowing.

"That's not important," Baldy mumbled. "He just told us to check on you. He said you've got an hour. He thought you might like the anticipation that statement brings. His words, not mine."

Skye let out a gasp and cry.

"What does that mean?" Cassidy asked.

"Let your imagination run wild."

And just as quickly as they appeared, they were gone.

Skye let out another cry and buried her face.

"It's going to be okay," Cassidy said, patting her friend's back. "We're going to think of a way out of this."

"I don't see how. It's not like either of us are secret ninjas or something."

Cassidy chomped down. She did have a few tricks up her sleeve. "We can't lose hope. We just need to think."

"I've been thinking for hours, and I'm still here."

Cassidy stood and began pacing the room. There had to be something they could do here. Something she'd missed. The last thing she was going to do was stay here like a sitting duck.

"Why do you look like you've done this before?" Skye's eyes followed her.

Cassidy shrugged, reminding herself to take it easy. "It's just adrenaline probably."

"Well, I've already searched the entire room. There's nothing here."

There had to be something. *Think, Cassidy. Think.*

Fight through the worst to get to the best. Another proverb from Lucy's Day-at-a-Glance. Why had that phrase struck her now? As a reminder not to give up, she realized.

Did Del keep that wisdom in mind while fighting cancer and trying to maintain her joy?

Cassidy would fight through this nightmare also, holding onto the belief that there was something better waiting for her in the future as well.

"Are those the same two men you saw before?" Cassidy asked, checking the bathroom cabinets.

"Yes. I have no idea who they are." Skye pulled her legs closer, her flowy flowered skirt stretched over her knees.

"You said the other man—the boss—that his voice didn't sound familiar?" Cassidy opened the door to the nightstand. It was empty. Of course, she already knew that because she'd looked there earlier.

"No, it didn't sound familiar."

"So we know that drugs are being smuggled and sold in the fruit at Buddy's produce stand," Cassidy said, thinking out loud. "It would make sense that Buddy is behind this. But you'd probably recognize his voice."

"Probably."

"Did it sound like Jimmy James?"

Skye swung her head up toward Cassidy. "No. Why?"

"He was helping to bring in produce for Buddy, off the books."

"Really? And I thought he was my friend. We actually went on a date once."

Cassidy paused. Jimmy James might be nice enough, but he didn't exactly seem like long-term relationship material. Nor did he seem like the creative free spirit Skye claimed she was looking for. "You know, Austin has been very concerned about you."

Skye frowned. "Austin is a great friend."

"That's all?" Cassidy checked the ledge above the door again. Nothing.

"What do you mean?"

Cassidy shrugged and ran her foot along the edge of the carpet. "Nothing. It's not important."

This wasn't the time to discuss love and romance. Cassidy just couldn't believe that Skye didn't know how much Austin liked her yet.

Nothing had been left at the edge of the carpet, so

Cassidy went back to the dresser. She opened a wooden box on top. Her eyes lit when she saw a phone inside.

A phone!

She held it up and showed it to Skye. But she didn't see the excitement she thought she would. Instead, Skye shrugged.

"It's mine, but it's dead. They just left it there to taunt me."

Cassidy nibbled on her bottom lip. Those men's wrong assumptions could be her salvation right now. "That might just be their biggest mistake."

"What do you mean?"

Cassidy glanced around the room. "I mean, I may be able to give this just enough charge to make a phone call."

———

Ty was trying not to be overprotective or overbearing. But Cassidy still wasn't answering her phone, and his gut told him that something was wrong.

Had she stumbled into something and not told him? Would she be foolish enough to go investigating by herself?

Ty knew Cassidy wouldn't approve of this, but he had a spare key to her place. He looked into things for the house's owner sometimes when Mr. Piedmont couldn't make it into town.

In order to make sure Cassidy was okay, Ty unlocked her front door. As he reached for the handle, he hesitated. He hoped Cassidy would forgive him for the intrusion, especially since it was borne out of concern and not curiosity.

Pushing aside his reservations, he opened the door and stepped inside. "Hello?"

No answer.

He glanced around before proceeding. Everything appeared in place, and no signs of a struggle were evident. That was the good news.

Carefully, he walked the perimeter of the great room. Nothing stood out as alarming, nor did anything give a clue as to where Cassidy had gone.

He hit each of the rooms. Again, nothing.

Maybe Ty was overreacting. Or maybe he was being too protective or even paranoid.

But he couldn't get past his gut feeling. That gut feeling had kept him and his guys alive.

Before he abandoned his mission, he went into the kitchen, near the phone. He'd had luck at Buddy's place finding that address on the pad of paper. Could something in this area indicate where Cassidy had gone?

He picked up a pad of paper and did the pencil trick again, running the lead over the blank page. Nothing appeared except for the number of a local pizza joint.

He opened the top drawer, and a phone book stared back at him.

He paused before sliding it closed.

Why did the bottom of this drawer look new and freshly painted? Mr. Piedmont hadn't been by lately to do any repairs.

It was probably nothing or a quick repair a renter had done.

Out of curiosity, he tapped it.

The drawer sounded hollow. Strangely hollow.

He opened the drawer below it, shoved aside some dish towels, and tapped the bottom of that one also.

They definitely sounded different.

Out of curiosity, he took out the phone book and examined that top drawer again. Using a knife from the rack beside the sink, he pried the bottom out.

It was a false bottom. And beneath it were four handguns.

Guns?

Did these belong to Cassidy?

The mystery surrounding the woman grew deeper.

As did Ty's concern.

———

Cassidy took out the battery from the smoke detector above the bed. It was a 9-volt. Perfect.

"What are you doing?" Skye uncoiled herself slightly from her earlier ball.

Cassidy had lost hope that her friend was going to be any help, though. The situation was making Skye shut down, and, at this rate, her friend would be catatonic before too long.

"I'm just trying something." Cassidy searched the rest of the room, looking for some type of wire or conductor. The lamp in the room had a cord, but she had nothing to cut it with.

"Cassidy?"

Cassidy paused for long enough to try and explain. "I . . . uh, I took a class once about how to charge a cell phone without a charger. Just in case."

"Sounds like a useful class."

Cassidy nodded. "It was."

It had been with the police force. She didn't share that.

"I have a battery, but I need something to get power from the battery to the phone."

"Like a wire?" Skye asked.

"Or even just a metal tip of some kind." She paced the room again, looking for something—anything—that she could use.

"How about this?" Skye reached for her ear and pulled something off.

Cassidy took the turquoise tassel earring from her. The piece had a long metal post. "You know? This might just work."

Skye suddenly came to life, no longer the limp rag doll sitting on the floor.

Cassidy's hands trembled as she worked the earring apart. She'd never actually done this—she'd only seen it done. But, in theory, it all made sense and was worth a try.

She had no other options right now.

Working carefully, she connected one end of the metal earring to the battery. She then let the metal touch the phone's port for a battery charger. She held her breath, waiting to see if it would work.

"We need to give it a few minutes," Cassidy said, resisting the urge to hold her breath.

"Those guys are going to be back any minute." Skye curled into her ball again.

Cassidy nodded, trying to keep her cool under pressure. "I know. I'm doing what I can. I promise."

"I know you are."

"Skye, if Buddy's not behind this, then who is?"

She shrugged. "Maybe it is Buddy. Maybe he disguised his voice."

"Why would he meet with you about doing a business deal? He would have just killed off the competition, don't you think?"

"Maybe when I walked into his house and saw the blood, I turned his plans upside down."

"If Buddy killed—or hurt—someone in his house, he would have disposed of the body and then returned to life as normal doing his undercover drug operation. Something must have spooked him."

"Maybe a competitor?" Skye asked.

Cassidy thought about it a moment before nodding. "Yes, that's a good possibility. Or someone he made mad. Maybe someone wanted to get even with him by using you instead."

Skye shivered. "The man who's keeping us here certainly seemed to know who I was. He even mentioned my friends who were investigating."

Cassidy shook off the thought. It didn't matter who was behind this right now. What really mattered was the two of them getting out of this alive.

"This is the moment, Skye." Cassidy stared at the phone with trepidation. If this didn't work . . . she didn't know what they would do.

She reached for the power button.

CHAPTER
TWENTY-SIX

CASSIDY HELD her breath as she waited to see if the screen would light up.

Please, please, please.

A moment later, the screen flickered. Then came on.

"It worked," she muttered, a rush of gratitude sweeping through her.

"What? Really?" Skye uncoiled and sprang toward her.

The battery only showed five percent. But Cassidy would take whatever she could get.

"If we're going to call someone, it needs to be now before this phone dies again." Cassidy began dialing.

"You're calling the police, right?" Skye said.

Cassidy shook her head. "No, I'm calling Ty."

"But . . ."

"Think about it, Skye. Do you want bumbling Chief Bozo or an ex-Navy SEAL?" Although they were out of Bozeman's jurisdiction, the man had left a bad taste in Cassidy's mouth for any law enforcement in this area.

"You're right. Call Ty." If the situation wasn't so serious, Skye's expression and quick agreement would have been almost comical.

Ty answered on the first ring. "Skye? Where are you?"

The concern was obvious in the tension of his voice. Just hearing Ty brought Cassidy an immense comfort.

"Ty, it's me. Cassidy. I'm with Skye, but we don't have much time. Someone grabbed us, and we're in a boat off the marina in Ocracoke. I'm pretty sure we're in a yacht at the end of the row here in the harbor—the most secluded spot—but I can't be sure."

"Are you two all right?" he rushed.

"Yeah, we're fine." Cassidy remembered the men's threat. "For now. But you've got to come help us. This phone is going to die in a minute."

"Anything else you can remember that will help me find you?"

"No, not really. These guys are armed, and they know what they're doing. They've been watching us, Ty, so they'll recognize you."

"You're on the boat right now?"

Cassidy glanced around, wishing she knew more. "That's right. I'm guessing we're in a room below deck. There are no windows. I don't think we're moving, but I can't be sure."

"I'm going to find you guys, Cassidy. Hold on until I get there."

"I'm trying, Ty." Just then, she heard footsteps coming down the hallway. "Come quickly. I've got to go."

She hung up and slid the phone between the mattresses, just in case they needed to use it again. As she did, the door opened, and two men stood there like executioners waiting to carry out their latest assignment.

"Someone could be watching us right now," Ty said, ducking behind an outbuilding at the harbor in Ocracoke.

He and Mac had gotten here surprisingly fast—in forty minutes, thanks to Mac borrowing a friend's speedboat.

Mac stood behind him, out of sight from anyone passing by. "I'll keep a lookout. We know no one followed us over in the boat."

"Another benefit to traveling by boat. The ferry would have taken too long."

Who was Ty kidding? It had already taken too long. A lot could happen in forty minutes.

He prayed that wasn't the case, and that Cassidy and Skye were okay.

Using his binoculars, he focused on the boat at the end of the dock. It was a large yacht—large enough that it could easily have an interior room without any windows.

But it was impossible to know for sure that was where Cassidy was.

As two people stepped onto the deck, Ty bristled.

"What is it?" Mac said.

"Someone just came out," Ty said. "One doesn't look like the type to own a boat like that. More like a hired thug."

"So you think that's our boat?"

Ty continued to watch. Though one of the men was big and burly, the other was on the shorter, scrawny side, but he carried himself like royalty. Why did the man seem familiar? Ty would have to get closer to figure it out.

Both of the men stood on the deck talking and staring

out over the water. As Ty looked more closely, he thought he saw a gun at the short man's waist.

"My gut tells me that's our boat," Ty said. "I'd like to know for sure before we develop our plan of action."

"If what you said is correct, those men would kill Cassidy and Skye before handing them over. We can't take that chance."

Ty hadn't wanted to say it out loud, but he agreed.

"When do you think the police will be here?" Mac asked.

"I called in that tip to them," Ty said. "I figure it will take them at least a couple of hours for them to figure it out. If we need them here sooner, we can call back."

The police would arrive with sirens blazing and guns drawn—which would only get the women killed. Ty needed to buy more time, so he'd called 911 to report two women had been abducted in Ocracoke, and that one of them had said something about being near the water. That should bring the police close enough to be ready if gunshots occurred, but there wouldn't be any of the urgency that might tip off the bad guys.

"A man after my own heart." Mac glanced at the yacht. "Let's say that's our boat. What's the plan?"

Ty's jaw hardened. "I'll go in the water and climb up the back side. They won't be expecting that. Then I'll find the ladies. I have a dry sack with a gun and my phone. If I don't come out in fifteen minutes, you definitely call the police for backup and give them more information this time."

"And then I go inside myself." Mac paused. "But you don't know what you're up against in there. We have no idea how many men are inside."

"There are two on the deck now. There could be more below. But I'd rather take my chances with you than I would trusting Bozeman."

"We're out of Bozeman's jurisdiction, but it wouldn't surprise me if he found a way to get involved," Mac said. "The good news is that the state police are pretty competent."

"But they won't get here in time. At least it's overcast, and we're only a few hours from sunset. The dark could work in our favor."

"We better get moving then. Because I have a bad feeling about this."

The two men didn't take Cassidy and Skye from the room. No, instead they'd tied them up, bringing in two wooden ladder-back chairs for the task.

With ropes securely around the women's midsections, the men stood at the door and stared at them. They'd announced that their boss was coming down to make an appearance.

And he had bad news. They had to do things his way or they'd both be killed.

"Who is this boss of yours?" Cassidy asked, praying that Ty would get help here soon.

Yes, praying. Funny what desperate times could make people do. But if praying and faith could bring Del joy in the face of cancer, certainly it couldn't hurt Cassidy now.

"Let's just say he's in the fruit business. The juiced-up kind."

Was it Buddy? Cassidy didn't think so. But if not Buddy, then who?

Something continued to nag at the back of Cassidy's mind—some sort of subtle detail that desperately wanted her attention.

Someone had wanted to make Buddy look bad. The only person that made sense was—

Just as the thought entered her head, a man stepped into the room.

She sucked in a breath.

It was just as Cassidy had suspected.

Sissy.

She should have known. The man had been observant —too observant. He'd been eating fruit every time she'd seen him—probably as a way to taunt them. He'd thrown suspicion off himself by calling the police on everyone who went near Buddy's place. Sissy had wanted Buddy to get caught and for his business to be shut down, so he could swoop in with his own drug enterprises.

But this Sissy wasn't the same bookish Sissy Cassidy had met earlier. No, this man's eyes had turned from frightened and uncertain to calculated and cold. Gone were his slumped shoulders and feeble movements. They'd been replaced by a cockiness that Cassidy had seen a million times before in criminals.

He smiled at Cassidy. "So we meet again."

The line sounded so Hollywood that Cassidy gagged a little. "So we do."

"I tried to get you to stay away, but you just kept poking and pushing."

She tugged against her restraints. "I'm not sure what tying me up will accomplish."

"You probably don't want to know." He smiled quickly before narrowing his eyes. "How did you find me?"

She couldn't exactly tell him she'd traced Skye's phone. "Someone saw my bike parked here and told me."

"Really?" Skye asked.

Cassidy ignored her, not wanting to explain any more than she had to.

"How fortuitous," Sissy said.

"I guess Buddy was too much competition for you, so you had to come and take him out. Only that blood the police found at his house wasn't his."

Sissy's eyes both lit and darkened, a disturbing combination as the man reveled in his own deviousness. "It belonged to one of my men who went to talk to him. It didn't go well."

"Where's Buddy now?"

"We took care of him. Don't you worry."

Cassidy continued to try and put the rest of the pieces in place. "You want to take his place by getting Skye to put drugs in her fruit?"

"That trick has already been done. We have other ways of getting our goods to the people who want them." He turned his nose up as if Cassidy had insulted him. "But I did propose that business proposition to Skye, to see her reaction."

"What makes you think you're going to get away with any of this?" Cassidy pulled against her ropes again. If she could just get them loose . . .

Sissy leaned down to face her. "Because I'm smarter than most people, and the East Coast is my domain and no one else's!"

"What are you going to do with us?" Skye's voice

cracked, and tears streamed down her cheeks. She'd been mostly quiet—but only because she was terrified.

"Now that you've seen my face, I have no choice but to kill you both. I know . . . it's quite unfortunate."

Skye let out a cry, and anger ripped through Cassidy. People who preyed on others who were weaker were the lowest form of scum.

"You didn't have to draw us out in the first place," Cassidy said. She needed to keep talking until Ty arrived. "Why did you ask Skye to come here?"

"I needed an unassuming contact in the area, and she fit the bill. Then you showed up and ruined everything." His guileless eyes locked onto Cassidy's. "Who are you really, Cassidy Livingston?"

Cassidy sucked in a breath. What was he talking about? Had she been made?

CHAPTER
TWENTY-SEVEN

"YOU KNOW my first and last name." Cassidy tried to keep the tremble from her voice and not give any indication how much Sissy's words had shaken her. "How?"

A soulless smile curled the corner of Sissy's lip. "I have my ways."

What if he was testing her? If he knew more than he let on?

Anxiety began clawing at Cassidy's gut. If he was at all connected with DH-7 . . . then she was a dead woman.

"That's right. I looked into you," he continued. "You don't have much of a history, do you? Simple Texas girl. College at Texas A&M, and you went on to work at an interior design firm afterward. Now, out of the blue, you're here. Are you the typical girl who wants to give up life in the fast lane to find herself on the sun-bleached shores?"

Thank goodness, Samuel had been thorough in covering all the bases.

"Maybe I am." She would have scoffed at the idea at

one time, but the longer she was in Lantern Beach, the more she understood how the ocean could be a balm to the heart.

"You don't even have credit cards."

She shrugged, remembering her cover. "My parents taught me not to go into debt."

He grunted. "Wise on their part."

As he stepped away, apparently satisfied for the moment, Cassidy released her breath. Maybe Sissy didn't know anything, and he was just trying to scare her.

"Well, this has been a nice little talk. But it's going to all be over soon." He nodded toward one of his men, who pulled out two syringes. "It's going to look like the two of you had a little accident. Had a little too much fun partying together with the drugs Cassidy found at Buddy's Produce stand."

"You knew about that?" How? Cassidy was observant. She hadn't been followed. She was certain of it. But that didn't mean someone hadn't been watching her.

"I know about a lot of things."

Her blood went a little colder. "People aren't going to believe we overdosed."

"No, but they might believe you overdosed while you were out boating and had a little accident." He smiled.

"It's doubtful."

"After we're through, they'll believe it," Sissy said. "I have rumors to start—rumors about Skye and her criminal past. I have syringes I can leave at both of your places, along with some of Buddy's fruit. I'll make it easy enough that even that police chief on Lantern Beach will put it together."

"You won't get away with it."

"You might be surprised. Either way we're going to wait until dark to make that happen, just to be safe. I'd advise you both to enjoy your last minutes of life." He glanced at the man flanking him. "Go ahead and help them relax."

As the man stepped toward Cassidy, instinct kicked in. No way was she taking more of that drug without a fight.

———

So far, so good.

Ty had managed to climb onto the back of the boat without anyone noticing him. He'd crept through a door and down the hallway unseen, using a towel he found on the deck to wipe up his wet footprints.

At the sound of voices in the distance, he slipped into a room. A closet, actually. He slid the door shut and waited, heart thumping in his chest.

His mind went back to his Navy SEAL days, to the missions he and his team had completed. Each one had been pulse-pounding and essential to the bigger picture.

Just like this one was. His friends wouldn't pay the price for someone else's evil plans.

The footsteps came closer.

"Did you check on number three?" someone asked.

That voice sounded familiar. Ty peered out the slit between the door and the frame.

It was . . . Sissy, Buddy Macklemore's quirky neighbor.

Sissy walked past with another man—a large one. But Sissy looked nothing like he did before. It was as if he'd transformed into a different person—probably because he had.

"He's sleeping like a baby," the man said. "And all the evidence is in place to make our plan work. The police have already discovered the knife we planted on Popeye's boat. We have Lenny heading over to Ms. Livingston's place now to plant the drugs and some invoices that will show she and Fuddy Duddy Buddy were working together. Everything is taken care of."

"Good," Sissy said. "As soon as it's dark, we start with the phase two of our plan. Rick and Steve are handling the ladies now, preparing them for their adventure tonight."

Fire burned in Ty's blood, and he gripped his gun more tightly.

He could shoot these men. He *wanted* to shoot these men. But if he did, he'd reveal his hand. The boat would erupt into chaos. That wasn't the way Ty preferred to do things.

Once the two men were out of sight, he crept from his hideaway and started down the hall again. He quietly eased himself down the stairs. More voices echoed in the distance.

Was someone . . . fighting?

He started toward the sound but stopped.

That wasn't a woman howling in pain.

It was a man. Two men?

He didn't know.

But something told him that Cassidy and Skye were okay.

As the door opened, he slipped behind the stairway. Two men emerged from a room in the distance. One rubbed his jaw and the other his forehead.

"That didn't go as planned." The bald guy muttered some not-so-PG words.

"Boss said we can't hurt 'em yet. Not if we want to maintain the cover story about how they died. Bruises would cause too much suspicion."

"That woman is a beast. Who would have thought a cute little blonde would have that much skill? I'd wring her neck if I could."

Were they talking about Cassidy?

Ty was about to find out.

As soon as the men climbed the stairs and passed by him, Ty rushed toward the room. A safety latch had been added to the outside of the door. He shoved it to the side and jerked the door open.

What he saw on the other side made his head swirl.

Cassidy and Skye were both tied to wooden chairs and struggled against the ropes around them. Their eyes lit when they saw him.

"You found us," Cassidy muttered.

"Of course I did." He rushed toward them, pulling out the knife from his belt. "But we don't have much time."

He untied Cassidy and then Skye. Skye threw her arms around him, clinging to him for life.

"Thank you," she whispered.

Cassidy only nodded appreciatively and rubbed her forehead. "I'm glad you got here okay."

He took a spare gun from his bag and slapped it in Cassidy's hand, anxious to see how she'd react. She didn't say anything, only waited. The woman was so purposeful sometimes it drove him crazy . . . yet it thoroughly impressed him at the same time.

"You ever shoot one of these before?" Ty asked Cassidy.

She nodded, her face not giving anything away.

"Good, because I don't know what's going to happen once we get upstairs." He took a step forward. "Stay behind me."

But before they could even leave the room, they heard footsteps coming down the stairs.

"You two, behind the bed," he ordered. "Now."

CHAPTER
TWENTY-EIGHT

CASSIDY BIT HER TONGUE, desperately wanting to help Ty, but knowing she had to be careful with how much skill she showed. If it came down to Ty's life or revealing she was a trained law enforcement agent, she was going to have to blow her cover. She couldn't live with herself otherwise.

It would mean a new place, a new home—but she'd think about all that later. Living was her top priority right now.

She knelt beside Skye behind the bed, hovering over her friend. She wasn't sure what was going to play out over the next few minutes. She could only hope for the best.

One of Sissy's men stepped into the room.

"What the—" he muttered.

Before he could say anything else, Ty wrapped his arm around the man's throat. The man struggled, trying to jerk Ty off of him. With his throat constricted, he couldn't speak. Couldn't cry for help.

Cassidy held her breath, trying to gauge when it was time to step in. Each of her muscles wound tightly, waiting to spring.

But she didn't need to.

The man slumped to the ground. Ty had knocked him out.

One down. Two more to go. At least, two more that Cassidy knew of, plus Sissy.

Ty motioned for them to follow him.

Skye's chest expanded and contracted too rapidly. Her eyes were glazed. She could pass out at any minute, Cassidy realized.

Just to be safe, Cassidy kept one hand on her elbow and, with the other, she shoved the gun in her waistband. They hurried from the room, Ty locking the man inside, and then rushed toward the stairs. Near the top, he motioned for them to wait.

A shadow passed by the entryway.

Sissy must have another guard waiting there.

Ty crept forward, using impressive self-control and fine-tuned instinct before grabbing the second man. Just as he'd done with the man downstairs, he wrapped an arm around his neck, cutting off the man's air until he slumped to the floor.

Ty nodded toward the hallway, and Cassidy and Skye rushed after him, stepping over the burly man on the floor.

Ty was good. Cassidy had seen a lot of maneuvers, but that wasn't one the police used regularly. She liked it. If Ty started shooting now, he'd tip Sissy off, and they needed the element of surprise. It would only help them right now.

The deck was just ahead.

But first they had to get past Sissy.

Ty stopped before they emerged and leaned closer. "If we can get to the back of the boat, we jump in the water and swim fast. The police should be here any time."

He scanned the area again.

"On the count of three, let's go," Ty said. "One. Two. Go!"

They darted toward the water, but, before they reached it, Skye tripped on her skirt. She hit the deck, the sound reverberating around them. Before Ty could grab her, Skye rolled, gravity pulling her farther down deck and away from them.

Cassidy froze, waiting for Skye to get her footing. She couldn't get to her in time without drawing more attention.

Before Skye could stand, a figure stepped from the cabin and jerked Skye to her feet. The thug put a gun to her head. "Don't move."

Everyone froze. Sissy stepped out behind him.

"Well, well," he said, clucking his tongue. "Look who we have here."

Seriously, this guy must have learned every line of his bad guy terminology from cheesy TV shows. And what kind of bad guy was named Sissy?

"Put your gun down," the thug muttered. "Or I'll shoot her."

Ty raised his hands and nodded. "Don't do anything rash."

"Put the gun down!"

Slowly, Ty lowered it to the deck.

Cassidy's gun was still in her waistband. He didn't

know she had it, and she needed to use that to her advantage.

"You three aren't going anywhere," Sissy said. "But you are going to make me do things the hard way."

"Just let us go," Cassidy said. "We won't tell."

Of course they'd tell, and everyone knew it. But she had to try using the excuse. The line sounded like something a rookie would say.

"I can't do that," Sissy said. "I should have just eliminated you from the start."

"That's a bad idea," Ty said. "You're going to get caught."

"I never get caught. You have no idea." A satisfied smile crossed Sissy's face. "You two certainly didn't suspect me, even after two visits."

"You put on a good act," Ty said. "But I already called the police. They'll be here soon."

"Quiet!" Sissy yelled, his nostrils flaring.

Skye gasped, the gun still pointed at her temple.

"Shoot her," Sissy said, glancing at his right-hand man.

"Shoot her?" the man repeated with wide eyes.

"Yes, shoot her. Can I make myself any clearer?"

"But . . ."

Before the man could say anything else, Sissy pulled out a gun and fired.

The thug clutched his chest and fell to the deck.

Skye screamed as Sissy grabbed her next.

"You know what I say? Eliminate the dead weight." Sissy turned to them. "Now, do I have your full attention?"

"Your guy is still alive," Cassidy said, needing to distract him. As Sissy looked at the man he'd just shot, she drew her own gun and pointed it at him. "Let her go."

Sissy nodded, as if impressed. "Clever. Very clever. But I'm not letting her go."

"This isn't going to end the way you want it to," Ty said.

"I don't know about that." The cockiness remained in Sissy's gaze.

Cassidy readjusted her aim at Sissy and resisted the urge to give him a steely-eyed stare. "You need to let us walk away."

He raised an eyebrow, a smile curling his lips. "You're tougher than I thought."

Stop acting like a professional, she reminded herself. Cassidy made the gun tremble in her hands, trying to act like she'd never used one. "Don't make me use this."

"You wouldn't."

"I would." She swallowed hard.

"That would make you a killer."

Sissy's words pierced her through the heart. She didn't want to be a killer. But maybe she already was.

She spotted Mac on the docks behind Sissy. He gestured wildly, and Cassidy tried not to stare.

The police, she realized. He was trying to tell her the police were almost here.

The problem was they might not have time for either the police or Mac to arrive.

"This is all a bad idea," she told Sissy, desperate to stabilize the situation.

"You've never seen a bad idea."

Oh, he had no idea.

"Just let the ladies go," Ty said. "I'll go with you."

"Too bad I don't want you." Sissy repositioned his gun against Skye.

Her friend let out another half gasp/half cry.

The situation was escalating, and Cassidy needed to do something before someone she cared about got hurt.

Her gun was locked and loaded. She had excellent aim. Every shooting instructor she'd ever had had told her that. If only she could get a good angle . . .

"You all need to go back downstairs." Sissy pointed with his gun. "Now."

Oh, no. No way was Cassidy going back down there. They'd never come back up. At least up here there was a chance for survival, for someone to see them and help.

"No," Cassidy said.

"Cassidy . . ." Ty muttered.

"I said go." Sissy pointed with his gun again. As soon as the barrel turned away from Skye, Cassidy fired.

She held her breath as she waited for the fallout.

Sissy screamed. Skye fell to the ground. Blood splattered on the floor and walls.

Cassidy rushed toward them as Ty kicked Sissy's gun away. The drug lord writhed with pain on the floor as blood poured from his hand.

She'd hit her target. His wrist.

And Skye was okay—other than the emotional damage.

Ty was okay.

That meant Cassidy was also okay.

At that moment, police flooded the boat.

This was all over. Finally.

CHAPTER
TWENTY-NINE

TY AND CASSIDY hadn't had a chance to talk since everything had gone down. They were ushered off the boat and questioned by state police. Finally, Ty, Cassidy, and Skye were left to gather their thoughts for a moment on a grassy area near the harbor.

The sun had set, but groups of people were still out, pausing in the distance to stare and speculate about what the excitement was about.

Just as Mac had suggested to Ty earlier, Chief Bozeman showed up. Apparently, neighboring police departments did help each other out around here.

In the distance, Buddy was led away in handcuffs. Sissy had kept him on the boat in another room, apparently. The police had enough evidence to put him away for a long time.

From what Ty had overheard the police saying, one of Sissy's men had confronted Buddy, and there'd been a fight. Buddy had run, but Sissy's men had found him, upset because Buddy had moved in on their turf. Buddy might not have been the biggest player in the room, but his crimes had been serious enough that he'd be going to prison.

Sissy's list of incriminating acts was even longer and darker. The man had a team of drug dealers up and down the East Coast, but Sissy's unassuming ways had allowed him to fly under the radar for far too long.

As the crowds began to thin, Ty glanced at Cassidy, remembering with amazement how everything had unfolded earlier.

"I'm glad you're okay," Ty said. "That was a risky move and an excellent shot."

Cassidy shrugged. "Beginner's luck."

"Well, it was impressive." But he wasn't sold on the beginner's luck part.

"Thanks for coming, by the way. I knew I could count on you."

"You can count on me anytime, Cassidy."

Her cheeks flushed, and she looked away. "It's good to have people in your corner."

"What happened in that room right before I got there?" Ty asked, watching Cassidy's face. "Those men looked beaten up."

Cassidy shrugged. "They tried to drug us, and we fought back."

Skye let out a harsh chuckle. "No, we didn't. I totally froze. But Cassidy swung her chair around—while she was still tied up—and hit the man in the head."

Ty's gaze went back to Cassidy. "Is that right?"

She shrugged again, not looking the least bit excited. "My adrenaline just kicked in. Adrenaline and instinct."

"She didn't stop there," Skye continued. "She slammed

her forehead into the other man and sent him reeling. I've never seen anything like it."

Ty's curiosity surged, but this wasn't the time to ask questions. And, even if he did ask, he was certain Cassidy wouldn't give him a straight answer.

From the corner of his eye, he saw someone approaching with a camera. Ernestine. As the octogenarian reporter raised it to snap a picture, Cassidy must have seen her. She pulled her hair into her face and raised her hand to block the shot.

Was Cassidy really that camera shy? She didn't seem like the type who worried about stuff like that. Then again, as he was constantly discovering, there was a lot about Cassidy Livingston he didn't know.

Right on cue, Mac came up and hooked his arm around Cassidy. "There's my girl. You're a tough chick, you know that."

"I'm not. Not really." Cassidy glanced over at Ernestine again and turned her back to her.

"You've seen more action in the crime-solving community in a month than Bozeman has the past two years," Mac continued.

"I guess I just have a knack for finding trouble."

"And you don't back down." He waved a finger at her, but his face beamed with pride.

"Maybe I just have good instincts." Cassidy offered a weak smile.

Ty could see the exhaustion on her face, but more so on Skye's. She wasn't the trooper that Cassidy was. "How about if we get you home? If you're free to go, of course."

"That would be great." Skye wrapped her arms over her chest.

Before Ty could consult with the police about it, a familiar truck pulled up, and Austin strode up a few minutes later. As soon as he reached Skye, she melted into his arms.

Thank goodness for this happy ending. Because things could have turned out a whole lot different.

———

Two hours later, Austin, Skye, Ty, and Cassidy sat in Austin's truck. Mac decided to stay with a friend in Ocracoke overnight. In the morning, another friend was coming to pick up the boat they'd borrowed, and then Mac would drive Cassidy's car back.

With Cassidy's bike loaded in the back of Austin's truck, they headed back toward Lantern Beach, silent at first.

Cassidy was grateful for the quiet.

She needed to distance herself from Ty, even though she wanted to be near him. She wanted to take his hand and fall into his embrace just like Skye had fallen into Austin's.

But she couldn't.

She feebly played with her purse strap instead.

Once on the ferry, quenchless darkness surrounded them. The clouds had temporarily cleared, and she could see stars.

And again, she wanted to fall into Ty. She wanted to pretend like they could have a relationship.

He shifted beside her, and his hand brushed hers. She couldn't look at him. If she saw his gaze, she'd forget everything her mind was telling her. Keep your distance, she reminded herself. Stay strong.

Something buzzed in her purse.

Her phone. Her secret phone.

It had to be Samuel. Had he discovered something new?

Her heart racing, she gripped her purse again. "I'm going to go stand outside for a minute. I could use some fresh air."

"I'll go with you." He grabbed the door handle.

She raised a hand. "Just . . . just give me a minute, okay? Please?"

He stared at her a moment, his eyes orbs of questions, but finally he nodded. "Sure."

Her heart sagged at his disappointment. But, sometimes, a girl had to make the hard choices. Painful choices. This was one of them.

Cassidy didn't like it, but she didn't have many options.

She slipped out and hurried away from the car, finding a lonely place near the railing. As the dark water rolled by, she closed her eyes, thankful that the water wasn't her grave. Not today, at least.

She found her phone and stuck it to her ear. Looking around once more to make sure she was alone, she put it to her ear. "Hey, Samuel."

"I have an update. I figured you'd want to know right way."

"What is it?" Was Cassidy a killer? She could hardly breathe as she waited.

"You didn't have anything to do with that woman's murder, Cassidy."

She released her breath before stopping suddenly. Had she heard him correctly? "How can you be sure?"

"We have another guy embedded with DH-7."

"What?" Why hadn't she heard about this before?

"The DEA has one of their guys in the gang."

Cassidy's spine straightened. "Who?"

"I can't tell you."

"Was he a part of it while I was undercover?"

"He was."

"And you didn't tell me?"

"It was important that no one knew," he said. "We thought if we kept it quiet, there was less chance of either of you being found out."

"But what if I'd needed him?" It didn't make any sense that they wouldn't share that information.

"Cassidy . . ." Samuel's tone made it clear he didn't want to talk about this anymore.

She swallowed hard and glanced around one more time. "What did he say?"

"Raul put that blood on you to test your loyalty. They were messing with your head, Cassidy. My contact assured me that you're innocent."

Relief made her joints feel like rubber. Despite the surprising and irksome news of another informant, Cassidy had never been so thankful.

She hadn't killed someone.

"Thank you, Samuel." She remembered the events of the evening. After a moment of contemplation, she filled him in on Sissy and flakka.

"Do we need to pull you?"

She glanced back at Austin's truck and remembered her friends there. Friends. It felt good to have people who had your back. Not because they worked with you or worked for your father. But because they cared about you as a person.

She wasn't ready to leave yet.

"No, I'm okay. I'll keep my eyes open."

"If anything changes, let me know."

"I will."

She slid her phone back into her purse just as Ty climbed from the truck and went to stand at the railing several feet down. He was trying to play it cool, but she knew he was keeping an eye on her. It was sweet.

She wove her way between cars until she reached him. Standing beside him, she leaned out on the railing and looked at the water.

"I know I've already said this, but thanks again for everything you did tonight," she started, wishing she could more adequately show her thanks.

"It was nothing."

She glanced at the moonlight hitting the waves, contemplating her next words. "You know, you've been a good friend since I came here. I appreciate that."

"I'd like to be more."

Cassidy closed her eyes as an internal war started within her. "I have a lot of things I need to work out, Ty."

He touched her shoulder and nearly made her lose her resolve. "Don't we all?"

She made the fatal mistake of looking up at him. Those eyes—full of expression—made her want to dive in. Instead, she threw her arms around his neck and pulled toward him for a hug. Ty wrapped his arms around her waist and held her close.

All her worries seemed to melt away, if just for a moment.

She'd thought she'd been such a good judge of character. But Ryan, the man she'd thought walked on water, had ignored her calls while hanging out with another woman. And Ty, a man she'd believed was a chauvinistic pig when they'd first met, actually had a heart of gold.

So much for her ability to figure people out.

She pulled away first, yet her hands rested on Ty's chest. She knew she should move them. But she couldn't. Or didn't. Or something.

She'd never felt so drawn to someone before.

"I need time," she said, staring at his lips instead of his eyes in an effort not to lose her resolve. "I don't know how much."

"I can give you time," he said.

"I don't . . ." Cassidy shook her head, at a loss for words. "I don't know how it's all going to turn out."

"What does that mean?" Questions and confusion etched into Ty's soft tones.

"It means . . ." She shook her head again, overwhelmed by her thoughts and emotions.

Ty leaned down to meet her gaze. "What aren't you telling me, Cassidy?"

Everything was on the edge of her tongue. She wished she could share it. Wished she could talk about it with someone. With Ty.

But that would put him in danger.

Besides, he'd made that call to the West Coast. He'd said it was to talk to his friend who was a SEAL out there. But this guy had been in San Diego—the same place that woman who looked like Cassidy had been murdered.

Cassidy wanted to believe it was a coincidence . . . but what if it wasn't? This was no time to be naïve.

She didn't say anything. She needed more time. Time to think. To be certain.

Finally, he stepped back, and Cassidy immediately missed his presence.

"I won't press you," he said. "When you're ready, you can let me know."

Gratitude filled her. "Thank you."

He wrapped his arm around her waist, and they walked back to Austin's truck. The ferry was about to dock. And Cassidy couldn't wait to get back home. Yes, home.

Funny how quickly Lantern Beach had earned that name.

~~~

Thank you for reading *Flood Watch*. If you enjoyed this book please consider leaving a review.

Keep reading for a preview of *Storm Surge*.

NOW AVAILABLE:
STORM SURGE

STORM SURGE: CHAPTER ONE

TODAY'S GOALS: CONTINUE LIFE AS NORMAL. SELL ICE CREAM. COOL IT WITH THE GOOGLE SEARCHES.

AS HAD BECOME HER ROUTINE, Cassidy Livingston stepped onto her deck just as the sun rose over the roaring Atlantic. She couldn't imagine not drinking in this view one day. The peacefulness of it helped her clear her head, gain her focus, and remind herself of her alternate personality.

Cady Matthews from Seattle, Washington, was gone. Cassidy Livingston of Lantern Beach, North Carolina, had taken her place.

Her old life seemed so far away from this island, where the sand had not only invaded her pores but her heart as well.

Cassidy had been on this isolated island for two months. She had four more to go. In some ways, that seemed like an eternity and in others it wasn't long enough.

Time shows us what's important.

She'd just been pondering that inspirational quote earlier, a nugget of wisdom from an old Day-at-a-Glance calendar that used to belong to her best friend, Lucy. The wisdom never ceased to be useful and relevant—especially since Cassidy came here to Lantern Beach.

"It's beautiful, isn't it, Kujo?" She glanced down at the golden retriever sitting beside her. He belonged to her neighbor Ty Chambers, but Cassidy was dog-sitting while Ty was out of town.

The dog nuzzled her hand in response.

"Days should start with pondering how big the world is and how small you are in comparison, right, boy?"

He barked in affirmation.

Cassidy took another sip of her coffee. As she scanned the shoreline, she paused and squinted. What was that?

Some kind of object had been beached a little farther down the sandy banks. From her perch atop her second-level deck, she couldn't make out any details, except that it appeared to be rectangular with blue and black tarps covering the edges.

She set her coffee on the railing, climbed down her exterior stairway, and trod over a patch of sandy cement before reaching the small path that cut over the dunes toward the beach.

As she passed Ty's house, she glanced over. He'd been out of town for six days, but Cassidy suspected he was home now. She'd seen a light on in one of his windows last night. It was hard to know for sure, since he hadn't taken his truck with him. Apparently, an old friend had picked him up.

A surprising jolt of sadness diced through her heart at the realization that he hadn't called. Their relationship was strange, one where they took two steps forward and one step back. But Cassidy had thought he'd call. Or stay in touch. Or do something to indicate he cared.

But the truth was, it was better this way. Ty had broken down her walls, and she'd been in the process of trying to restore them. Ty didn't know who Cassidy really was, and when he found out . . . she had no idea what he would think.

Car tires rumbled behind her, and Cassidy paused. A moment later, Serena Lavinia jumped out of her rundown Ford Fiesta and rushed toward Cassidy. Today, the woman-of-many-faces was dressed like a preppy boarding-school girl in a button-up top and khaki shorts. Serena always kept Cassidy on her toes with her ever-changing personalities. The girl took "finding herself" to a whole new level.

Cassidy motioned for Serena to join her on the narrow path to the beach. As she crested the dune, a strong breeze hit her. Even when it was 90 outside, this breeze made it feel 20 degrees cooler. That worked out well in the summer, but she couldn't imagine the place during winter.

"I was hoping I'd catch you," Serena said, joining her on the sand. "I wanted to ask if I could take an earlier shift today."

"Why's that?" Cassidy kept walking, and Serena joined her.

"I have a story to cover later for the paper, and the person I need to interview is only available at three. It's the organizer of the Fourth of July parade."

Fourth of July was three days away, and apparently Lantern Beach liked to celebrate big. There was not only a parade here on the tiny island, but also concerts by local musicians and church groups, an art show, and even a 5K.

"That is exciting." Cassidy said. "I'm glad you're enjoying all your jobs so much."

Serena worked part-time for Cassidy, part-time at her aunt Skye's produce stand, and part-time as a beat reporter for the local island newspaper.

"So . . . about the shifts?" Serena asked, raking her dark hair from her eyes as the wind hit her.

"I don't mind if we switch," Cassidy answered.

It wasn't like Cassidy had anything better to do on the island, a fact that normally drove her crazy. For as long as she could remember, her whole life had been filled with purpose, and to-do lists, and twelve-step plans on how to move ahead. She'd always been an over-achiever, and it was eye-opening trying to simply be an ice cream woman now.

Cassidy glanced again at the mystery object, which was only eight feet away now. What could that be? Something from a ship? A temporary shelter that had blown down the beach? Part of Blackbeard's treasure?

As she reached the structure, she saw it was six feet long and three feet wide. Was that a boat? Maybe a raft some kids had made? She had trouble picturing children putting this together. The vessel was too . . . complex.

Her gut churned. There was more to this. An ominous feeling hovered over her as she peered above the edge.

"What is this?" Serena wrinkled her nose at what looked to be a pile of trash.

Cassidy squinted. "That's what I'm trying to figure out."

"It looks like a boat."

"It does, doesn't it?" Cassidy continued to stare at the

wreckage. She felt sure that's what it was—something the ocean had eaten up and spit back out.

The sides of the structure were comprised of Styrofoam that had been duct-taped in place. The frame was some sort of metal. Bottles and snack wrappers littered the bottom of the craft.

Her apprehension churned harder.

"This is crazy," Serena said, jiggling the side. "But it's pretty sturdy."

Cassidy picked up something inside. She sucked in a breath at what she saw.

It was a cloth. And it was bloody.

People had been on this contraption. People who were hurt or injured.

This hadn't been a peaceful adventure. No, this had been a life-or-death mission.

Cassidy pulled out her phone. She needed to call the police. Now.

Click here to continue reading

ALSO BY CHRISTY BARRITT:

BOOKS IN THE LANTERN BEACH UNIVERSE

LANTERN BEACH MYSTERIES

The series that started it all! When a notorious gang puts a bounty on Detective Cady Matthews' head, she has no choice but to hide until she can testify at trial. But her temporary home across the country on a remote North Carolina island isn't as peaceful as she initially thinks. Living under the new identity of Cassidy Livingston, she struggles to keep her investigative skills tucked away. One wrong move could lead to both her discovery and her demise.

#1 Hidden Currents
#2 Flood Watch
#3 Storm Surge
#4 Dangerous Waters
#5 Perilous Riptide
#6 Deadly Undertow

LANTERN BEACH ROMANTIC SUSPENSE

Standalone romantic suspense novels that fear a pulse-pounding story centered around beloved Lantern Beach residents.

Tides of Deception
Shadow of Intrigue
Storm of Doubt
Winds of Danger
Rains of Remorse
Torrents of Fear

LANTERN BEACH PD

When a cult moves to Lantern Beach, the whole island is in upheaval. Police Chief Cassidy Chambers must find answers before total chaos erupts.

#1 On the Lookout
#2 Attempt to Locate
#3 First Degree Murder
#4 Dead on Arrival
#5 Plan of Action

LANTERN BEACH BLACKOUT

Join a group of Navy SEALs who've come to Lantern Beach to start a private security firm. But a secret from their past may destroy them.

#1 Dark Water
#2 Safe Harbor
#3 Ripple Effect
#4 Rising Tide

LANTERN BEACH GUARDIANS

During a turbulent storm, a child is found on the beach, washed up from the ocean. Making matters worse—the girl can't speak.

#1 Hide and Seek
#2 Shock and Awe
#3 Safe and Sound

LANTERN BEACH BLACKOUT: THE NEW RECRUITS

Four new recruits join Blackout, but someone is determined to teach them a lesson.

#1 Rocco
#2 Axel
#3 Beckett
#4 Gabe

LANTERN BEACH MAYDAY

Kenzie and Jimmy James work on a luxury yacht chartering a dangerous course.

#1 Run Aground

LANTERN BEACH CHRISTMAS

Catch up with your favorite Lantern Beach characters as they come together to help the town's beloved police chief.

Silent Night

LANTERN BEACH BLACKOUT: DANGER RISING

A new team is formed to combat a new enemy. The mission puts everyone on the line, and failure will mean certain death.

BEACH BOUND
BOOKS AND BEANS MYSTERIES

When widow Tali Robinson moves to Lantern Beach to renovate an old oceanfront store and turn it into a book-store/coffee shop, the last thing she expects to find is a human skeleton hidden within the walls. But her troubles don't stop there, and before long she realizes she doesn't have to dig for trouble, she's bound to run into it.

ABOUT THE AUTHOR

USA Today has called Christy Barritt's books "scary, funny, passionate, and quirky."

Christy writes both mystery and romantic suspense novels that are clean with underlying messages of faith. Her books have sold more than three million copies and have won the Daphne du Maurier Award for Excellence in Suspense and Mystery, have been twice nominated for the Romantic Times Reviewers' Choice Award, and have finaled for both a Carol Award and Foreword Magazine's Book of the Year.

She is married to her Prince Charming, a man who thinks she's hilarious—but only when she's not trying to be. Christy is a self-proclaimed klutz, an avid music lover who's known for spontaneously bursting into song, and a road trip aficionado.

When she's not working or spending time with her family, she enjoys singing, playing the guitar, and exploring small, unsuspecting towns where people have no idea how accident-prone she is.

Find Christy online at:
www.christybarritt.com

www.facebook.com/christybarritt
www.twitter.com/cbarritt

Sign up for Christy's newsletter to get information on all of her latest releases here: **www.christybarritt.com/news letter-sign-up/**

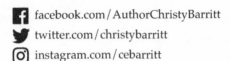

facebook.com / AuthorChristyBarritt
twitter.com / christybarritt
instagram.com / cebarritt

Made in United States
Orlando, FL
27 May 2024

47257229R00161